# PREGNANT BY MY BEST FRIEND'S HUSBAND

## WRITTEN BY:

## NATIONAL BESTSELLING AUTHOR,

## MZ. BIGGS

**PREGNANT BY MY BEST FRIEND'S HUSBAND**

Published by Cole Hart Signature, LLC.

**Check Out These Other Great Books By Mz. Biggs:**

See What Had Happened Was: A Contemporary Love Story (Part: 1-3)

Yearning For The Taste of A Bad Boy (Part: 1-3)

Dirty South: A Dope Boy Love Story (Part: 1)

Falling for A Dope Boy (Part: 1-3)

Feenin' For That Thug Lovin' (Part: 1-3)

A Bossed Up Valentine's (Anthology)

Jaxson and Giah: An Undeniable Love (Part: 1-2)

Finding My Rib: A Complicated Love Story (Part: 1)

In love With My Cuddy Buddy (Part: 1-2)-Collaboration

Your Husband's Cheating On Us (Part: 1-3)

From Cuddy Buddy To Wifey: Levi and Raven's Story (Standalone/Collaboration)

In Love With My Father's Boyfriend (Standalone)

Your Husband's Calling Me Wifey (Standalone)

She's Not Just A Snack... She's A Whole Buffet: BBWs Do It Better (Standalone)

Blood Over Loyalty: A Brother's Betrayal (Standalone)

Married to the Community D (Part: 1-2)

Downgraded: From Wifey to Mistress (Part: 1-3)

# Pregnant By My Best Friend's Husband

A Mother's Prayer (Part: 1-2)

Heart of A Champion... Mind Of A Killer (Standalone)

Turned Out By My Husband's Best Man (Standalone)

Ain't No Lovin' Like Gulf Coast Lovin' On The 4th of July (A Novella)

This Is Why I Love You (A Novella)

The Hood Was My Claim To Fame (A Novella)

A Killer Valentine's (Anthology)

Tantalizing Temptations in New Orleans (An Erotic Novella)

Santa Blessed Me With a Jacktown Boss (Novella)

Diamonds and Pearls (Standalone)

Dating A Female Goon (Standalone/Collaboration)

### *Author's Acknowledgements:*

I'm baccccckkkkk...lol. It's been a while since I last dropped a book, but I promise I came back swinging with this one. It's always imperative that I thank God for keeping me covered through this journey as an author and allowing me the opportunity to continue to push out books. I'm 46 books in and none of this would be possible without Him.

To my fiancé, Darnell Rhyme, you have been amazing to me through this journey. When I dropped the ball and was ready to give up on writing, you never gave up on me. You kept pushing me until I was able to see what I was missing, and I was ready to pick the pen up again. I'm glad that you were able to see how passionate I was about writing, and you were willing to motivate me to keep going, even when I felt like I wanted to quit. I love you so much, and I can't wait to be your wife.

To my three amigos (the Biggs' Kids-De'Miktric Jr., Allanah, and Kaiden). You are the greatest blessing that I've ever received. You are the reason that I continue to grind and work to make sure I can give you a life better than I ever had. Please know that I love you and everything that I do, I do for you.

To all of my readers and supporters, you don't know how grateful I am for you. I had someone reach out to me the other day about a book that I wrote when I was two years in the game. I had completely forgotten about the book, but she sent me a review that she'd recently left that had me in tears. It's those moments that push me to go harder. I appreciate each and every one of you and I thank you for continuing to rock with me, even when I wasn't dropping books the way I started off. Trust me, that consistency is back and I'm ready to bring you something fresh and better than I've ever written before.

All I ask is that you please take the time to leave an honest review on either Amazon or Goodreads after reading the book. Your support is greatly appreciated. Also, feel free to reach out to me anytime via the contact information listed below. Happy Reading... ☺

~Mz. Biggs

### *Want to connect with me? Here's how:*

Email: authoress.mz.biggs@gmail.com

Twitter: @mz_biggz

Instagram: mz.biggs

Goodreads: Mz. Biggs

Facebook: https://www.facebook.com/authoress.biggs

Author Page: https://www.facebook.com/MzBiggs3/

Look for my Reading Group on Facebook: Lounging with Mz. Biggs

### *Chapter One:*

*Porscha high-stepped out of the elevator onto the fifth floor where her husband's office was located. Turning her nose up at the few patrons that sat scattered in the waiting area, she pranced like a horse to his secretary, Angelique's, desk. Angelique was on the phone when Porscha reached her, but that didn't bother Porscha at all. She stood at Angelique's desk, tapping her long-pointed fingernails on top of it, waiting to be acknowledged. She knew Angelique saw her standing there and was just ignoring her, but she wasn't about to let that happen. She hated being ignored, but not as much as she hated waiting. So, she started popping her lips real loud to irritate Angelique.*

*"May I help you?" Angelique practically slammed her phone down on her desk to address her.*

*"Do you know who I am?" Porscha quizzed, not appreciating the fact that Angelique was getting sassy with her.*

*"Who doesn't know who you are?" Angelique paused. Porscha's eyes remained trained on Angelique. She saw her abruptly roll her eyes.*

*"You trying the wrong one, lil' girl," Porscha aggressively spat.*

*"Lil' girl? I understand that Michael is your husband, but I work here, and you will respect me. Now, may I help you?" Angelique spoke through clenched teeth. She kept a straight expression on her face and crossed her arms across her chest.*

*"You work here now, but if you keep giving me attitude, you'll be out that door faster than you can blink," Porscha shot back. A small smile crept across her face. She turned around to view everyone in the waiting area. She wanted to see if anybody was going to pat her on the back for putting Angelique's rude ass in her place. When nobody said anything, she instantly refocused her attention on Angelique.*

*"Before I can blink, huh? You mean like this?" Angelique taunted Porscha by relentlessly blinking her eyes. She even winked at Porscha when she was done. Porscha wanted to knock the smirk off her face, but she knew she couldn't fight her inside the office. "Again, may I help you?" Angelique spoke.*

*Porscha knew she wasn't getting anywhere by going back and forth with Angelique, so she decided to go ahead and tell her what she wanted. She made it a point to give her major attitude when she spoke to her.*

*"You may help me by telling my husband that I'm here to see him," Porscha replied, looking around the waiting area once more. She bucked her head forward like someone that was about to barf at the people sitting around. To her, none of them looked as if they could afford the type of houses that her husband was known for selling. Shit, some of them looked like they were homeless to her. They could've at least dressed themselves up a bit, she thought. "Oh, and please let him know*

that he needs to come out of the office immediately," she added.

"He's in a meeting. Please have a seat, and I'll let you know when he's available," Angelique informed her with the same smirk on her face.

"You can wipe that lil' funky smirk off your face. I'm not about to sit and wait on him to come out of a meeting; tell him I'm here, and I need to see him now," Porscha insisted, pounding her fist on the desk. Her eyes turned red, and her breathing increased. All eyes were immediately on her as she acted out of character. Porscha was known for acting bougie at times, but she was too upset to be classy today. She didn't give a damn what people thought of her in this present moment. She'd just been embarrassed at her favorite store, and she needed him to answer for it. She didn't understand how two of her credit cards declined when they both had high limits, and Michael swore to her that he paid them both off last month when she got a call saying that the payments were past due.

"I understand that you are here to see him; so are these other people that are sitting over there, patiently waiting for him to come out of his meeting. You're more than welcome to sit over there and wait, or I can call security. Which would you prefer?" Angelique snidely commented.

*This bitch got me all the way fucked up, Porscha thought to herself. She was going to get in that office to see Michael with or without Angelique allowing her to do so.*

*"Fine. I'll wait," Porscha announced with a smile on her face. "I'm sorry for my outburst," she stated with a sly smirk that Angelique hadn't noticed.*

*Porscha made Angelique believe she was about to go take a seat in the waiting area, but she had other plans. She waltzed over to the burnt orange modern wingback chair that was closest to her. The six-inch heels of her red bottoms clicked across the floor with every step she took. Several thoughts ran through her mind as she contemplated over what she was about to do. Reaching the chair, she sat her purse down on it before kicking her shoes off under the chair. She waited good until Angelique had picked the phone back up and was in a deep conversation before she took off running down the hall toward the conference room.*

*"Hey, you can't go back there." She heard Angelique yell out from behind her, but that didn't stop her.*

*When Porscha reached the conference room, she tightly wrapped her right hand around the doorknob and roughly pushed it opened. The door hit the wall so hard, that it bounced off the wall and went flying back toward her. She was barely able to duck inside before the door hit her. The conference room was filled with men and women dressed in blue and black business suits. There was some type of presentation going on that apparently her husband was not a part of because when she skimmed the room in search of him, he was nowhere to be found amongst the group of people.*

*"Shit!" Porscha loudly muttered; she dropped her head in embarrassment.*

*"Hey, Porscha; we are kind of in the middle of something. Everything okay?" Jared, one of Michael's co-workers asked. He walked over toward her to see what was going on. She couldn't even look him in the eyes when she spoke to him.*

*"Sorry, I was looking for my husband. Have you seen Michael?" Porscha spoke as if she hadn't done anything wrong. She was trying to play off the fact that she was ashamed of her actions.*

*"Well, he's not in here. Did you try checking his office first?"*

*"His secretary said he was in a meeting, and this is normally where he has meetings, so that's why I came in here first. But, I'll go check his office now. Thanks!" Porscha smiled and walked away, trying her best to not make herself look any crazier.*

*"Are you sure everything is okay?" Jared stopped her to inquire. Porscha could hear the sincerity in his voice, but there was no way she was going to tell him the real reason she was there acting so belligerent.*

*"Never better," she replied to him over her shoulder, as she commenced to prancing back down the hall toward Michael's office.*

*Standing in front of Michaels' door stood Angelique with security. Angelique had a mean mug on her face. Her arms were yet again crossed over her chest, and she tapped her foot on the floor. It was obvious that she was awaiting Porscha's return. By the look on their faces, Porscha was fully aware that they meant business and was not about to play with her. She had to play her cards right if she didn't want to get kicked out of the office.*

*"What is going on?" Porscha asked when she made it where Angelique was standing. She was trying to play off what she'd just done.*

*"I told you that Michael was in a meeting. You've come up here more than anybody and know how he doesn't like to be disturbed when he is in meetings. That's why I told you that you would have to wait. You agreed to wait in the waiting area, yet, you ran like a banshee down to the conference room and interrupted another meeting that was in progress. Now, either you are going to leave on your own, or I will have security escort you out of here," Angelique sternly instructed Porscha with her finger pointing toward the door. Porscha was even more embarrassed and didn't know what to do. Never had she*

imagined she'd be in the situation that she was in and wanted badly just to wrap her hands around Michael's neck.

"I'm not leaving until I see my husband," she barked. She was furious and was not about to let Angelique, security, or anyone else deter her from what she came there to do.

"Do what you have to do," Angelique announced to security and walked away.

Porscha shrugged her shoulders and braced herself. She looked between the front door and the door security was blocking. They were the doors to her husband's office, and she was determined to get in there.

"This is all a big misunderstanding. You see, I'm Mrs. Alexander, wife of the best damn real estate agent in the south. All I want to do is have a moment to speak with my husband and I'll be on my way," she told them. She hoped that by telling them that she was his wife, they'd let her pass. She didn't even understand why they were giving her such a hard time considering she'd been to his office on several occasions and everyone should've known who she was.

"We understand that, but he's not able to see you at the moment. We're going to have to ask you to leave," one of the security guards informed her. She sized them up and down before reading the names on their nametags. They were new, but she didn't care. They were going to newly be out of a job once she told her husband how they treated her.

"Fine," she shouted. "Assholes!" She muttered to them before turning to gather her belongings. She slid her shoes back on her feet and held her purse in her hand before marching toward the elevator to leave. The guards walked closely behind her on her walk of shame to leave. Before anyone knew it, Porscha kicked her shoes off again, spun around the guards and made a dash for Michael's door. Imagine her surprise when she got there, and the door was locked.

**Bam... Bam...**

She profusely kicked on the door until she felt herself being lifted up in the air. The security guards retrieved her while Angelique picked up everything that belonged to her. They didn't even wait on the elevators to arrive to take her out of the building; they took the stairs. That's how bad they wanted her gone. Porscha kicked and screamed the entire time.

"You will hear from my lawyers," she yelled at them as they sat her on the ground in front of the building. "All of you will be fired. You hear that? Fired! Especially you, bitch!" she angrily spat, peering into Angelique's eyes. Angelique chose not to respond to her. However, she threw her purse and shoes out the door behind her. The guards stood in front of the door so that Porscha couldn't get back inside.

Porscha got up and dusted herself off. She wanted to sit outside and wait on Michael to come out, but she didn't want them to call the police on her. What she couldn't understand was if her husband was in the building, why he wouldn't come out of his office? He had to have heard her in there. She got ready to walk to her car but was in awe when she saw it being dragged onto the bed of a tow truck.

"Hey, what the hell are you doing with my car?" she asked the tow truck driver.

"I'm just doing my job, ma'am. This car note hasn't been paid in three months, and the finance company sent me to pick it up," he explained to her. At least, that was what he was trying to do until she started popping off at him.

"That's a mufuckin' lie. My husband pays my car note every month. You need to check your fuckin' paperwork again," Porscha barked, snatching the paperwork out of the man's hand.

"Ma'am, there's no need for name calling. Now, what you can do is back the hell up and let me take a look at things." The man yanked the information back out of her hands and put it to where only he could see it. He wanted to be sure that he had the correct name and was not in the mood to be arguing with some scorned woman. "Are you Michael Alexander?" the man asked her.

"Do I look like a damn man to you?" Porscha barked.

"You can never tell these days. Damn men be dressed up like real women out here." The man chuckled. "Now, is your name Michael Alexander or not?" the man asked again. Porscha knew *he was doing it to be funny, so she just went along with it. If that's what she had to do to get what she wanted, then she was willing to do it.*

*"That's my husband, but what does that have to do with anything? This car is in my name. I've been driving it for the past year," she remarked. That time, she tried to be a lot nicer because it would take her a lot further than snapping on the man.*

*The overweight man peered at her before struggling to go up the ramp that now housed her car. She could see him taking deep breaths and heavily sweating. He took the back of his hand and wiped the sweat from his forehead. Porscha frowned when she saw him wipe that same hand across the front of his pants. She thought it was nasty for people to wipe anything on their clothes. The man looked down at her and she threw a fake smile on her face. She didn't want him to know that she was looking down on him or else he might not have helped her.*

*"What's your name?" she asked, hoping to break the silence between them.*

*"Tim," he nonchalantly replied. She stopped talking because clearly, he was mad about having to go up the ramp.*

*Porscha watched as he marched toward the front of her car. He stopped right past the driver's door and pulled his thick glasses from the top of his head, allowing them to rest on the bridge of his nose. Examining the papers in his hand and the*

VIN in the front windshield that appeared to have been altered, the man did his best to confirm that he indeed had the correct car.

"I'm going to have to call this in," Tim informed her.

Tim marched back down the ramp; he was clearly annoyed about something. Porscha looked at him and laughed because as usual, she perceived that she was right, and he was wrong. He was picking up the wrong car and when he put it down, it better not have a scratch anywhere on it, she thought to herself. If anything, he'd better hope that she let him go without making him apologize to her in front of the people that had started circling around to see what had happened. But, after a few moments of the man being on the phone, she saw her car continuing to roll onto the back of the truck. Tim struggled with climbing on the ramp again to get to the car. He bent over and rested his hands on his knees to regain control of his breathing once he'd reached the car.

"You okay?" Porscha asked, appearing concerned. She really wanted to ask why the fuck he hadn't let her car back down yet, but she bit her tongue.

"I got this," Tim replied.

"Okay." Porscha shrugged her shoulders and continued to observe Tim.

After some time, he stood straight up and moved back over to the driver's side of the vehicle. He slithered a Slim Jim in by the *window to pop the lock. It happened so fast, Porscha didn't get the chance to tell him to be careful with her shit.*

*Tim yanked the door open and studied the label stuck on the side of the door. Evidently, he was able to identify the car as the correct car that he was looking for because he slammed the door, hopped off the truck and pushed right past Porscha, bumping her in the process. Porscha stood by the truck in shock. Her mouth hung open and there was nothing else she could say.*

*The truck roared as Tim drove away with Porscha's beautiful, candy apple red Mercedes C300. The people standing around her didn't make anything any better. She turned and peered back at the building one last time. She felt hopeless. She glanced up at the frosty window she knew to be her husband's office window, hoping she could see him. It wasn't until she turned back to face the street that she laid eyes on her husband as he sped past her with another woman occupying his front seat. He wouldn't even look at her as he drove by.*

*Within a blink of an eye, Porscha's life had changed. She couldn't understand what she'd done to deserve the luck she'd received that day. She tried running behind Michael's car and calling his name, but it was to no avail. He was gone.*

"Aaaaagggghhhhh..." Porscha screamed as she woke up from her deep slumber. She grabbed ahold of her chest and felt around her bed. Michael was sucking the paint off the walls with his snoring. She felt safe for the moment. But in the back of her mind, it appeared that a storm was brewing. Nobody had nightmares like that for nothing, right?

### Chapter Two:

Porscha could not go back to sleep and couldn't understand how Michael could still be asleep, especially after she had woke up screaming. She was annoyed because she felt like he was purposely ignoring her, and that was something she didn't tolerate.

Porscha grew up in the projects. Up until she was thirteen years old, people used to tease her because she would always go to school smelling like piss. She had a problem with her bladder that would cause her to pee in the bed. Her mother got so sick of washing her sheets almost every day, so she made it a point to sometimes send her to school without making sure she took a bath first. Porscha never understood why her mother would do her like that, but she never questioned her.

Through those years, Porscha grew to hate her mother. She avoided being around her at all costs. It wasn't until she graduated from high school that her mother even attempted to show her an ounce of love or that she was even proud of her. That was when Porscha decided she was no longer going to be the person that was picked on and ridiculed. She was going to make it where she became successful in life and make her mother and everyone else regret the day that they ever doubted her.

It wasn't until she was in college that she met her husband, Michael. At first sight, she thought he was one of the better-looking men that she'd ever laid eyes on. He was over six feet tall, which she loved. Besides, she lived by the motto that a man had to be six feet or taller to take her for a ride. If you get the drift. He had a light skin complexion, yet his hair and eyes were jet black. The best thing about his hair were the 360 waves that he rocked. However, Michael wasn't an athletic or muscular build. He was slender, but she loved how his demeanor demanded respect. Everything about him screamed money to her, and that was what the only thing that caused her to consider talking to him because there was still something about him that she was not attracted to. It had to be the fact that when she noticed him across the room, before they were introduced to each other, she peeped out that he talked too damn much. That was something he continued to do today. She'd gotten used to it and learned how to tune his ass out when she didn't want to hear what he had to say. If it wasn't about money, their marriage, or finding a way to grow, she really didn't have time for shit that Michael or anyone else had to say.

Porscha attempted to lie back down, but she couldn't sleep. She wanted to talk about her dreams, but she really didn't have anyone to talk to about them. She had a best friend named, Keyanna, that lived in another state, but it was too early to call her, and Michael was playing possum on her ass. She hated to wake him up, but she was determined to make someone hear her out.

Feeling unsure of herself, Porscha jaggedly shook Michael to wake him up. How the hell could he still be sleeping after she'd woke up screaming? There was no way he didn't hear her. He must've just been playing possum because he didn't want to go through another night of hearing about her eerie dreams.

"Why the hell you shaking me like that?" he grumpily entreated, slowly opening up his walnut-shaped eyes. He rolled over to lay eyes on her. "I told you the last time you had one of those crazy ass dreams to not tell me about the shit. You good. I'm good. We good. And our shit is good. It's almost as if you want something bad to happen to us." He turned back over so his back would be facing her.

"You keep saying that, but these dreams aren't occurring for no reason. And why the fuck would I want something bad to happen? You're an idiot just for saying that dumb shit," she gawked before shaking him again. "Get up, now, Michael," she demanded.

When he didn't move, she threw her arms together across her chest and gazed at him with one of the ugliest pouts she'd ever made. The time on the clock on Michael's side of the bed read 1:23 a.m., and she was pissed. It was going to be another long ass night for her, and she hated that. She had shit to do and needed to get as much sleep as she could.

Porscha had to be up early the next morning to meet with a potential client for a makeup consultation, and she knew that the lack of sleep would only make her agitated, and she didn't want to go into a meeting with a foul attitude. That would be a sure way of losing money.

"I know what will get your ass up," she announced before stretching her arm as far as it would go. When she couldn't reach what she was aiming for, she leaned over in the bed. She was almost spooning him the way her body was position. She wrapped her arm around him and laid her hand on his stomach.

"Stay just like that and sleep will hit you soon," Michael instructed. Porscha rolled her eyes because she wasn't trying to hear that shit. It didn't take a rocket scientist to figure out sleep wasn't going to hit her any time soon. That was how it always was after one of her terrible dreams. She thought about calling her best friend, Keyanna, but she was a new mother, and she didn't want to disturb her any more than she thought the baby was probably already doing.

Slowly, yet cautiously, Porscha eased her hand down from Michael's stomach to his dick. She was moving leisurely because he was just like her when he didn't get a good nights' rest. He didn't care if it was because he was hanging out late or if they had a late-night sex session, he still needed to be able to get at least six hours of good sleep or he would raise hell for the entire day. But, Porscha knew what she needed to get some sleep, and she was willing to fight for it that night.

"What are you doing, Porscha?" Michael asked with an attitude.

"You know damn well what I'm doing, and you know damn well what I want, so you might as well turn your raggedy ass on over and let me get what I need before I take it," she seductively insisted. She was almost shocked to see Michael turn over without putting up a fuss like he would any other time. That was one of the many things she hated about him. He was stubborn as hell.

"Just call me drain-o while you watch me drain this dick dry," she told him and slithered on down to where her face was between his legs. Slowly, she began licking and kissing on his thighs since his boxers were still on. Glancing up, she could see his dick beginning to rise, and she smiled knowing that she was about to go on the ride of her life.

Porscha wasted no time pulling his dick out of the hole that was in the center of his boxers. She positioned herself on her knees and opened her mouth as wide as she could before devouring all of him inside of her mouth.

"Damn..." Michael groaned while heavily breathing. He placed his left hand behind his head and his right hand behind her head, enjoying everything that Porscha was doing to him. You would've thought his ass was Hugh Hefner by the way he was lying there.

Porscha slowly bobbed her head up and down on Michael's dick, paying close attention to his mushroom shaped tip. She went all the way down a few times before flicking her slippery tongue around the tip. Small speckles of spit trickled down from her lips, creating a stream of moisture around the shaft. Moving her hands in a jerking motion up and down his dick helped to lubricate it. Michael used the hand that he had behind her head to gently massage her scalp while his pre-cum made its way up to her tongue. Porscha's panties instantly became soaked, and she was ready to receive him inside of her. Michael was only seven inches, but his width made up for everything that he lacked in inches, and his stroke game was on point, most of the time. He was the reason she began to believe that size really didn't matter.

Full of excitement, she wasted no time removing her panties before she positioned herself to where she was still squatted but on her feet and did a duck walk forward. She swiftly inserted his fully erect dick inside of her and pulled her gown over her head to remove it. She exhaled the moment she started sliding up and down his pole. The feelings Porscha felt were unreal. For once in their relationship, riding his dick wasn't doing anything for her. She rolled her eyes and turned her body around to the reverse cowgirl position.

"What are you doing? You know I don't like when you ride it backwards. I like to look into your eyes," Michael seethed.

"Can you let me do me?" she irritably insisted. She'd quickly became agitated and uninterested, but she didn't tell him that. Instead, she continued riding him backwards, rubbing her clit at the same time. It was sad, but that was the only way she'd be able to get her nut.

Intensely, she moved her fingers between rubbing on her clit and stroking his balls. He loved whenever she played with his balls. It would also make him cum quicker. She wished she didn't have to think that way, but that was her truth.

"Grrrrrr..." She listened as he growled behind her. That was an indication that he was on the verge of getting his nut and there was no way in hell she was going to allow him to get his and she not get hers. Porscha began grinding on his dick; that would drive both of them over the edge.

Within a matter of seconds, they both came. Porscha jumped up and went straight to the bathroom. Michael shot up in the bed like the Undertaker. She could see him scratching the top of his head with a confused expression on his face through the mirror that sat adjacent to their bed.

"Damn, you just gonna get up like I didn't just make you feel good?"

"You didn't. I did all the work," Porscha sassily snarled.

"What? Do you know how much concentrating I had to do to keep my dick up?" Michael hissed, clearly feeling some type of way with her.

Porscha heard what he said but didn't feel the need to address it. However, she changed her direction of travel. Naked as the day she was born, she pranced through the house as if nothing were wrong, headed straight to the kitchen. As soon as her foot hit the cold floor, she rethought the dumb idea she had to leave out of the room undressed; she should've at least put her house shoes on. The kitchen was freezing to her. That was because the way the air was set up in the house, most of it blew to the front of the house where the kitchen was located.

"Porscha?" Michael called out to her, but she ignored him.

Opening the cabinet, she pulled out a big pot and put it inside the sink. She twisted both water knobs to the on position, hoping to quickly fill the pot up.

"I know you heard me calling you," Michael barked, walking in the kitchen as well. He at least thought to put his slides on. But, his dick was still hanging out of the hole in the front of his boxers. It was limp and freely swinging. "What are you doing? It's still dark outside!" he exclaimed.

"I got hungry. Go back to bed," she insisted.

"What the hell you about to eat that requires this much water?" he inquired before going over to the sink and turning the water off.

"I'm about to boil some eggs."

"What the hell you need all this damn water for? It ain't Easter."

"And what does Easter have to do with anything?"

"You actin' like you bout to boil eggs for a damn Easter Egg Hunt. What is wrong with you?"

"I don't know. I keep having these dreams, and you don't want to hear about them," Porscha explained. "I just want to know what they mean."

"I know, but I can't tell you what they mean. Maybe Keyanna's ass is broke," Michael stated, coming up with anything that he could in hopes of making Porscha feel better.

"Why would Keyanna be broke? They have their own construction company. Devon makes a ton of money!"

"And how would you know that? We tell people shit all the time and they believe us. Who's to say that they haven't been lying about what they have?"

"Keyanna wouldn't lie to me. She's never had a reason to," Porscha hollered. She was furious at Michael. Her hands flew up on her hips and she intently stared at him. The tension between them was so thick that it could be cut with a knife.

"Come on, Porscha. Let's just go get back in the bed. We can even go for a round two," Michael implied, winking at her. He thought he was helping the situation, but he only made things bad for himself. He'd just reminded Porscha of the smart ass comment he made about having to concentrate to keep his dick up to fuck her. She was mad all over again.

Porscha pushed him out of the way and grabbed the pot that was almost filled to the brim. She proceeded to put it on the stove. She placed it on the big eye in the front and turned the knob on high, so she could boil the water.

"Michael, go to bed. Don't you have meetings and shit in the morning? You need all your sleep, so you don't have to work so hard to concentrate!" she emphasized. He was so in awe with the way she was moving around after their sex session, that he didn't realize what she'd said.

"Whatever. I'm not about to let you fuck up this high I'm on. I needed that nut," he commented and turned and headed back toward the bedroom. Porscha paced back and forth in the kitchen as she waited on the water to finish boiling. She looked in the cabinets for something she could snack on while she waited.

The cabinets were nearly empty, so she tried the refrigerator. It was almost as empty as the cabinets. She couldn't believe that she'd been so busy with school and trying to build her own business that she'd forgotten to take care of her duties in the house like cooking, cleaning, getting groceries, and doing the laundry. She made a mental note to put all of that on her to-do list. Keyanna and Porscha used to argue at times about Porscha talking about a to-do list because there were times when

Porscha was so exhausted. Keyanna told her all the time that she should ask Michael for help, but she never did. Porscha remembered when they got married, she told Michael that she wanted to work from home, so she could be one of those 'back in the day women.' The kind that didn't work and took care of home. The sight of the bare cabinets and refrigerator proved to her that she wasn't meant to be that kind of woman.

When she checked the water in the pot, she could see the bubbles starting to form in it. That was good enough for her. She turned the stove off and grabbed two pot holders. Sliding her hands inside of them, she grabbed the pot off the stove and marched toward her bedroom. She had to take her time walking because she didn't want any of the water to hit the floor and she surely didn't want the water to burn her.

Michael had left the bedroom door open, which was perfect for Porscha because that meant she didn't have to put the pot down just to open it. She waltzed inside the room and without warning, closed her eyes and threw the water on the bed while yelling, "Concentrate on this!"

"What the fuck are you doing?" Michael roared from behind her. Porscha opened her eyes and turned toward Michael. She was furious that she didn't check to see if his ass was in the bed before she wasted all that damn water that she'd worked hard to get nice and hot for his ass.

"I was trying to make a hot sausage, but your ass wasn't in the bed," she growled at him, looking down at his limp dick.

"What the fuck? What were you trying to do?"

"I was trying to help you concentrate, nigga!"

"You were about to burn me with some hot ass water over a comment I made trying to be funny? Really, Porscha? Is this what our relationship has come to?"

Porscha shrugged her shoulders and walked away. She didn't even bother to take the pot back to the kitchen. She dropped it on the floor and continued to walk toward the guest room that was across the hall from their room.

"Your ass is going to clean all this shit up. You hear me?" Michael walked behind her, scolding her like she was his child. She shut the door in his face and crawled into the bed. "I don't know what's going on with you, but you need to call somebody. I'm calling a damn therapist on your crazy ass tomorrow. Better yet, I'm going to have my momma come up here. She's going to be hotter than fish grease when she learns that you tried to kill her baby. I bet her presence will make your ass snap back in line," he continued.

"Fuck you and your bald headed, no edge having mamme. She bring her ass in here on some bullshit and you'll both be dead." Porscha couldn't stand Michael's mother, and she made that known to any and everybody that would listen.

To Porscha, Michael's mother never saw fault in anything that he did. If they got into it and he ran to his mother, which he did often, she'd call Porscha like she was checking her. Porscha always shut her down. The day Michael married her was the day she became number one in his life. *He gon' fuck around and they be sharing a plot*, Porscha thought.

"What is your problem with my mother? She loves you like you are her daughter."

"Boy, if you don't go somewhere with that lying. You trying to get us both struck down?" Porscha asked, amused at the fact that Michael would rather lie than tell the truth. She didn't know who was worse with the lying; him or his mother.

"Fine, I'm calling Keyanna then," Michael asserted.

Keyanna was like Porscha's sister, but she hadn't seen her in well over a year because she was too busy 'living her best life.' She missed her friend and would love to spend time with her. Maybe she'd be able to help her figure out what all those bad dreams meant.

"Damn, you gonna call Mother Theresa too?"

"You're not funny, Porscha!"

"Whatever!" Porscha yelled before finally closing her eyes. She laid still and prayed that sleep would find her soon.

### *Chapter Three:*

Michael was still highly upset when he woke up the next morning. Not because Porscha woke him up in the middle of the night for sex, but because she tried to burn his ass up. It wasn't a secret that things had gotten bad between the two of them, but he didn't realize they were that bad. She told him it was because of the comment that he made about concentrating to keep his dick up, but in his mind, there had to be something else. Besides, he was only joking with her. Had he known that she would've taken things to the extreme, he would've kept the joke to himself.

Sleeping on the couch was not his best option, but it was his only one. Since their bed was soaking wet and she'd taken over the only guest room that was suited for someone to sleep in, the couch was his only choice.

Michael handled his hygiene and got dressed before he went in search of Porscha. He searched all throughout the house for her. When he found her in the kitchen, he paused before stepping inside of there. He peeked over at the stove to see if it was on before he actually entered.

"We need to talk," he stuttered.

"Talk about what? I know you not about to bring that shit up about your momma coming to visit again. She's not welcomed in my house," Porscha sternly hissed.

"This is not just your house and as long as I breath, my mother will be welcomed anywhere that I am. You need to get rid of that funky ass attitude and stop thinking you run shit. I wear the pants around this mufucka," Michael angrily retorted. Porscha never once turned to make eye contact with him, and he hated that. He was always taught that if someone was talking to you, you needed to turn around and listen to every word that they said so you wouldn't miss something important. He didn't understand why his mother would tell him that when most times, he figured that all people did was lie, and he wasn't interested in those lies.

"Don't press your luck with me. You know it ain't shit for me to tell you to get your dusty dick ass out too."

"I'm not about to keep entertaining that bullshit you're talking. You better put some mufuckin' respect on my mother's name too," he roared. Michael stood back and noticed Porscha starting to move around the kitchen. She went under the cabinet and took out one of the saucepans. Michael wasn't stupid; he figured she'd try to burn him again which was the reason he didn't get too close up on her ass. "You got me fucked up if you don't think I'll make you eat your damn teeth. Throw some hot water on me if you want to and I promise you won't do the shit to no one else."

Porscha continued on with her movement. Michael observed everything that she was doing. Immediately, when he saw her going toward the stove, he darted out of the kitchen. Michael loved the hell out of Porscha, but not enough to let her cause him bodily harm. She was never the person that he'd imagine would do something so ratchet. He thought about how perfect Porscha was to him. She stood about five feet and two inches tall. She was like a small dog with a big bite. Her caramel colored skin ways always glowing, and her dark brown eyes always shined bright. She was smart as hell and very ambitious. That was what made him fall in love with her. One thing Michael quickly learned about Porscha was that she could be mean as fuck, sweet as candy, cold as winter, evil as hell, or loyal as a soldier, all depending on how a person was with her.

She'd been having the same fucked up dreams for the past three months. He kept telling her to go see her therapist because therapy always helped her in the past, but Porscha made it clear that she didn't want to hear that.

"Michael?" Porscha called out to him.

"What?" he replied in a loud tone.

"Come again..." she requested. This time, she had her hand resting on her left hip. She damn near stared him down. He already knew what that meant. He'd fucked up by hollering at her. He noticed her eyebrow raise, so he softened his tone.

"What is it, Porscha?"

"That's what the fuck I thought," she mumbled. "Come back in the kitchen so I can fix you some breakfast," she requested.

She had a smile so big plastered on her face that Michael instantly became nervous.

"Fuck that!" he squealed and headed toward the front door. "I'll stop at McDonald's on my way to work. Matter fact, I'm not even hungry; I'm on a diet," he lied.

"Damn, can I at least get a kiss goodbye or something?" Porscha closed her eyes and puckered up her lips. She was antagonizing him and pushing him to want to put his hands on her. If she wasn't careful, she was going to get exactly what her ass was asking for. After a few moments of waiting for that kiss and it never happened, she began to speak. "That's fine. Make sure you hurry home from work; I'll have dinner ready." Michael snapped his head so hard looking back at her. She must've thought he was a damn fool. There wasn't enough tea in China that would make him eat her cooking or go in a kitchen with her while she cooked.

"Porscha, don't get fucked up!"

"What I do now? I'm just trying to cook for my man after all of that good dick you gave me earlier this morning; I think you earned a homecooked meal," she commented, prancing toward him with a big ass grin on her face.

Michael didn't trust that shit. Porscha was acting as if nothing happened. He was trying his best to go along with it because he didn't want to fuck his mind up before going into his meeting, but the way she was acting had him nervous as hell. Porscha walked smooth past him and over to the blinds in the living room. She opened them up and stared out of them for a while before she turned around and looked at him.

"Have you noticed that white van over there?" she asked, pointing at the van that was parked across the street from their house.

"What white van?" he queried, moving over next to her so that he could see out the blinds as well. They didn't have to hold them open with their fingers because they opened wide enough on their own, so they could very discreetly see the van without anyone knowing that they were watching.

"I saw it two nights ago when I was coming home, and it's out there again today," Porscha explained.

Michael became nervous. He'd seen more than enough movies to know that when there was a suspicious vehicle popping up, something was about to go down. *Was there some kind of meaning behind Porscha's dreams?* he questioned himself.

"It's probably nothing," he said, trying to persuade her into thinking everything was okay. "I'll see you later," he told her before carrying out his normal routine of placing a kiss on her cheek and walking out of the door toward the garage.

Inside the garage, Michael slid inside of his car and closed his eyes for a brief moment. A strange feeling came over him as he started the car and opened the garage to back out. When he was safely on the street and driving away from his house, he felt better.  He kept looking up in his rearview mirror to see if the van was following him.  When he got off the street and noticed that there was nothing behind him, a sense of relief came over him.  He used that time to call Keyanna to talk to her about Porscha.

"Bitcccchhhhh... What you up to, boo? It's been forever since we talked. The baby's getting bigger by the day, and you've been MIA. Plus, I can't wait to 'bust down, Keyanna' on my baby daddy's dick in a few weeks." Keyanna cheerfully started rambling through the phone the minute she picked up.  She freely spoke the way they always did whenever one of them called the other. Michael removed the phone from his ear and frowned at it after hearing Keyanna talking about sexing Devon's buck-eyed ass.

"First of all, I'm not your bitch. Secondly, I don't care what you and that lame do," Michael grumpily stated.

"Huh? Fuck you calling my phone for?" Her attitude immediately changed.

"Well good morning to your ass too," Michael commented, giving her back the same attitude she'd given him.

"Look, don't be on the line that I pay for running up my unlimited minutes with your bullshit.  Fuck you on my line for?" Keyanna asked again.

"You're pushing me to say something I might regret, Keyanna. I'm only calling you for Porscha, but you about to make me come to Mississippi and put this size 13 in yo' ass."

"You come right on down here and see won't yo' ass leave with this size seven in yours. I may have just had a baby and my pussy out of order, but these hands not. Fuck around and catch these hoes," Keyanna snapped back.

"Keyanna, shut the fuck up and listen. This why I don't like dealing with you or that no good nigga of yours."

"How you know he no good? Is he paying your bills or laying it down in your bedroom? I think the fuck not, so don't be disrespecting him." Keyanna was giving Michael the business and a headache at the same damn time. He roughly rubbed the temple of his head and rethought the fact that he even called her about seeing Porscha. There was no way he'd be able to stay in a house with Keyanna or Devon for more than a few hours without wanting to hurt their asses. "Stop holding the phone; speak nigga!" Keyanna directed.

"The only reason I called you was for Porscha. I don't like y'all just as much as y'all don't like me, so you should know that it took a lot for me to even make this call," Michael explained.

"You know I'll do anything for my girl. However, you or no one else will disrespect me or my man. What is it that you want?" Michael looked at the phone again and was about to say something out of line to her, but he kept his negative comments to himself because he really was sincere in his reasons for calling.

"Look, I don't know if she's told you or not, but she's been having these bad dreams lately. I'm not sure if it's because she miscarried or she's under a lot of stress with school and starting her company. But, is there any way you can talk to her? Better yet, can you come visit? I'll cover all of your expenses," Michael asserted. He crossed his fingers, hoping that she'd go ahead and say yes since she said that she'd do anything for her friend.

"My baby is barely two months old. I don't know how Devon would feel about me just up and going on a trip like that," Keyanna advised him.

"You can bring his ass too," Michael implied, gritting his teeth. He didn't like Devon because he thought Devon thought too highly of himself. For whatever reason, whenever they all got together, him and Devon always clashed and damn near get into a fight. But, he was willing to be the bigger person if it meant helping Porscha get in a better place. He desired to regain the feelings he had for her when they first got together.

"You know my husband don't like your ass," Keyanna pleasantly told him. "He don't even like hearing your name, so I know it's going to take an act of God to get him to agree to be anywhere near you."

Michael's relationship with Keyanna was nowhere near as bad as his relationship with Devon was. But, he didn't like the way that Keyanna was always so damn blunt. She didn't try to say shit in a nice way at all. With her, you were always destined to get the one hundred percent truth.

"The feeling is mutual. But I really need you to do this for me. If not for me, do it for Porscha. She really needs you. Besides, she's missed out on so much in the last year, that it would be great for the two of you to be back together again." Michael did his best to persuade Keyanna into agreeing to visit.

"Fine, I'll talk to Devon and see what we can do. But, I'm not making any promises, and if he says no, then that's that! I don't go against my husband for nobody." *Didn't this bitch just say she'd do anything for her friend,* Michael thought.

"Yeah, we all know that. He probably be beating your ass too," Michael muttered. He didn't realize he'd said it aloud until Keyanna started snapping off on him.

"Excuse me," Keyanna spoke. "Let me tell you something, Michael Fuck Nigga Alexander. I know a good man when I see one, and my husband is definitely that. He goes to work every day and comes home to me every night; he makes sure all the bills are paid, that we have all of our basic necessities and that I don't have to want for nothing. Not only that, I can peacefully sleep without worrying about him trying to run behind the next bitch. I may not go to church, but I know the Bible well enough to know that the man is supposed to be the head of the household. Therefore, whatever my husband says, go. I'd be a fool to go against my husband for a man that doesn't pay attention to what his wife needs or anything else." Keyanna ended the call without giving him a chance to respond.

"Fuck!" Michael bellowed to himself before punching his steering wheel. He knew how protective Keyanna was over her husband, so he knew he should've chosen his words wisely. He wanted to call back to apologize but didn't want to make the same mistake twice. So, he sent her a text instead.

*Michael: Sis, I'm sorry for being an ass. I really do need you here for Porscha. She's going through something and I don't know what it is. If you want me to call Devon, then I will do that as well. Please help me out! Love you, Michael.*

Michael sat still for a moment, trying to collect his thoughts. His stomach churned as he typed out the text because he had to suck up his pride to be nice to Keyanna. He thought about going ahead and calling Devon, but he felt as though Keyanna would come through for him. He just hoped she didn't call Porscha and get her all worked up.

*Beeeepppppppp...*

Michael looked up when he heard someone blowing their horn at him and realized that the white van that was across the street from his home was behind him. Instantly, sweat beads started forming on his brow. His hands started trembling beyond his control. His breathing became erratic until he saw the van drive around him.

"Get your shit together," he told himself before gradually putting his feet on the gas and driving toward his office.

### Chapter Four:

Hanging up the phone with Michael, Keyanna stood and went to go check on her baby. She'd just put him down to sleep, but she was still very careful with him. It seemed like she was checking on him every five minutes because of how common it was for babies under six months to die from Sudden Infant Death Syndrome (SIDS).

DJ was peacefully sleeping in his crib. Keyanna smiled at him before making her way into the kitchen. It had been a while since she'd been able to cook breakfast for Devon, so she figured she'd surprise him. Especially, since she was already up and didn't have to worry about the baby.

Sitting the baby monitor on the counter, she went to work pulling out her pots and pans. She was going to do some French toast with eggs and bacon and cut up some fresh fruit on the side. She was proud of herself for even feeling motivated to want to cook after the lack of sleep she'd gotten lately. But, it was also her way of getting Devon to agree to go see Porscha with her.

"Good morning, baby," Devon greeted her as soon as he walked in the kitchen. He wrapped his arms around her from the back and kissed the back of her neck.

"The hell you preach. Don't come in here starting shit knowing we can't have sex for another week," she told him, laughing.

"I know, but you are just so damn sexy to me. I love you so much," he expressed, turning her around to face him.

"I love you too," she cooed before they exchanged a passionate kiss.

"I don't know what I've done to deserve you, but you better bet I'm going to keep on doing it. I'll never leave room for another man to come in and take my spot," he advised.

"You'll never have to worry about that. I want you and only you," she responded. "Now, go have a seat, and I'll fix our plates," she told him.

Devon walked around the island in the middle of the kitchen and decided to take a seat on one of the bar stools. Keyanna never took her eyes off him as he walked away. She loved everything about her husband. He was six feet even in height, had naturally curly hair that he still liked to wear in a mohawk; his mocha colored flawless skin, his succulent lips, and the way his body was made up gave her chills. Devon didn't go to the gym, but the muscular frame of his body would give anybody the illusion that he did. He was her own personal version of Method Man. The only difference was that he didn't have any facial hair. That was by her request, of course. Facial hair was not something that she was very fond of.

Keyanna loved Devon's drive. He went to college to be an architect and ended up with his own construction company. When Keyanna was in college, she was undecided on what she wanted to be, so she majored in early childhood education only because she loved children. However, when she graduated, she got a job as a substitute teacher, and when she saw how bad the little kids were, she quickly changed her mind. She went to the nearest community college and majored in paralegal technology. She worked part-time at a law firm until she had DJ. With all of the videos floating around on social media of nannies beating on kids and how kids had been dying at daycares, Keyanna knew there was no way in hell she was going to let anybody watch her son. At least, not until he was old enough to talk and tell if somebody did something to him that they weren't supposed to be doing. So, Devon and Keyanna decided together that she could be a stay-at-home mom, and she had loved every minute of it.

"You okay, baby? You staring at me like you want me to come over there and do something to you," Devon told her, snapping her away from her thoughts. She looked over at him and smiled.

"Can't I just adore God's work," she cornily replied. Devon couldn't do anything but laugh.

"Hurry up and come sit your fine ass down next to me," he told her.

"Give me one sec. You sure you don't want to sit at the table?" she asked.

"Naw, this is fine. You are sitting down with me, right?"

"Yes, baby. Plus, I need to talk to you."

"Damn... I knew there was a reason behind you cooking." He laughed. "Let me finish getting dressed, and I'll be right back," he told her. That was fine with her because that would give her time to actually prepare the food.

Twenty minutes later, the food was done and waiting on Devon. "Baby, where are you?" Keyanna called up to him.

"I'm on my way," he replied right as he was walking back into the kitchen. "You acting like you missed a nigga," he teased and took a seat back at the island.

"Whatever, big head." She sat their plates down and playfully swatted at the back of his head before sitting down next to him.

"So, what's up?" Devon got serious.

"Calm down; it's nothing major. Michael called me this morning."

"For what?"

"He said that he thinks Porscha is going through something, and he wanted to know if we could come up for a visit. I know that you are working, but I'd really like to go see her. She's been so busy with school and working on her company, that she missed out on our anniversary party, baby shower, and the birth of DJ."

"What does that have to do with me? You know I can't stand Michael's lame ass," Devon protested. "That nigga have me wanting to knock his fuckin' socks off while he still in his rundown ass shoes," Devon admitted. Keyanna damn near fell out of her chair laughing at his ass.

"You a whole damn fool." Keyanna beamed. She found herself in a trance, staring at Devon. There was nothing she didn't like about him; which killed her that she'd been keeping a secret from him. One that would ultimately rock their whole world.

"Ole fuck boy ass nigga," Devon snarled. Keyanna immediately snapped out of her trance.

"I know, baby. But this isn't about him; it's about Porscha, and if she needs me, I have to be there for her. Besides, he said he would cover all of our expenses, and we wouldn't have to get a hotel because we can just stay at the house with them."

"I'm glad he said that he would cover the expenses, but I have my own money; I don't need shit from him or any other nigga. Furthermore, you know damn well I'm not staying under the same roof as him. That nigga still look like he piss in the bed." Devon chuckled, but Keyanna didn't laugh. She was more concerned with Devon not wanting to stay at the house. There was no way she could take her baby to a hotel at such a young age.

"What about the baby? A hotel is entirely too small to take everything that we need. Plus, I have to be able to pump my breast, heat the milk, and do everything else I need for the baby, and I'm not trying to be stuck in a little space." Keyanna was trying her best to persuade her husband to agree to the visit.

"I just don't know. What is he saying is going on with Porscha?" Devon asked, finally showing an ounce of concern.

"One of the things he's saying is that she's been having nightmares. He didn't say what they were about, but I know something has to be up because me and Porscha talk about everything, no matter when we talk. For her to not have told me about any nightmares, that worries me."

"You really think something is wrong with her? Maybe she's just tired of his ass." Devon tried to joke again but stopped when he realized that Keyanna was not laughing. "My bad, babe. If it means that much to you, we can go. Now that I think about it, we haven't been anywhere in a while, so Memphis would be a great idea. And it's a free trip. Hell, yeah we going."

"What happened to you not wanting anything from another nigga?" Keyanna teased.

"This is different. If he wants to pay me to look in his uglass face and damn near whoop his ass, then so be it," Devon spoke before pouring syrup on his French toast and chomping away at his food.

*That was easier than I thought,* Keyanna thought to herself before she started eating as well.

### Chapter Five:

Devon got up from eating and went to put the plates in the sink. "I'll load the dishwasher while you go check on DJ," he told Keyanna.

"Okay," she said and left out of the kitchen.

Devon went to the entryway of the kitchen that was next to the living room to make sure Keyanna was out of sight before pulling his cell phone out of his pocket. It had been going off left and right, but he was talking to Keyanna loud enough to where she wouldn't hear the vibrations in his pocket.

*Work: Why haven't you called me this morning?*

*Work: I miss you!*

*Work: I really wish you'd leave her so we could be together.*

*Work: You promised me that once she had this baby, you'd feel more comfortable leaving that bitch. If you don't leave her like you told me then we are going to have a lot of problems.*

Devon had been dealing with another woman for the past year or so. He couldn't even explain why he was doing it. He loved everything about Keyanna, but when she got pregnant, things in their relationship seemed to change. He should've felt blessed to have DJ, but he told Keyanna when they first got together that he didn't want any children. She told him that she would remain on birth control, and he even used condoms when they had sex, despite the fact that they were married; he wanted to remain safe. However, they got drunk one night, and he slipped up. He'd been kicking himself in the ass ever since.

Keyanna was gorgeous to him and surely the woman of any man's dreams. She was fun-sized with her four feet nine-inch height. Keyanna was very health conscious and monitored everything that they ate. She weighed no more than a buck twenty-five, soaking wet; it didn't take long for her to drop the thirty pounds she put on after giving birth to DJ. He loved the fact that their hair was similar in the way that she had natural curls as well. Keyanna's hair was way thicker and longer than his. Her high cheekbones, dark mysterious eyes, and smooth skin always made him think that she should've been a model. The only thing that was stopping her was her height and dark-colored skin.

Devon and Keyanna met through a mutual friend when they were in college. He was not interested in being in a relationship and thought their first date would lead to a one-night stand; that was how mostly all of his other dates ended. But, Keyanna was different. They went out to eat and spent the rest of their night talking. Even when he drove her home, he immediately called her on his way back to his apartment and they talked until they both fell asleep on the phone. He knew then that she would be different and seriously wanted to date her. They'd been inseparable ever since then.

Devon knew that having a baby would cause a rift in their relationship. He hated the fact that he was having to share the attention he was used to receiving with someone else. He never talked to Keyanna about it, but it really bothered him. Then, she would have moments where she didn't want to be intimate during the pregnancy because she said he wasn't gentle, or he would cause her pussy to swell. Shit, that was what he thought he was supposed to do. Make that pussy swell so he knew he was doing it well.

**Work: Why are you ignoring me?**

Devon's phone continued to go off, and it was starting to annoy him. He had to save the girl in his phone under 'work' because he knew that if she called while he was with Keyanna, Keyanna wouldn't think to question him about it.

**Devon: Stop blowing up my damn phone. I'm with my fuckin' wife.**

**Work: But you need to be here with me. I miss you. I want to feel you inside of me.**

Devon's dick instantly rocked up. He picked up the phone and called the woman's number. He stayed in the doorway of the kitchen, so he could see or hear when Keyanna was coming and could change the conversation to make it seem as if he was really talking about work.

"Hey, baby," she happily greeted him.

"Why are you doing this shit, Alex? You already know that I'm married, and you're just somebody I fuck with from time to time. You can't be blowing my shit up like that. Don't start that shit!"

"Nigga, I don't know what the fuck you thought this was. This not no pump and dump situation. You fuck me when you want and gon' about your business. That's not how I get down, and you know it. Besides, you promised we would be together, and I need you." Devon had to look at the phone for a minute. *Is this bitch being serious right now?*

"Well guess what, she needs me too. And so does my damn son."

"I don't give a damn about her or him. All I want is you. Where that lil' ugly ass baby at anyway?"

"Bitch, don't fuckin' play with me. Don't ever disrespect my seed again," Devon spoke through clenched teeth.

"You don't even want the baby. How can you make me get an abortion and you let her keep that lil' monkey?" Alex angrily asked.

"I know yo' mufuckin' cheese done slid off your cracker. You got me all the way fucked up if you think I'm going to sit on this phone and let you keep talkin' shit about the lil' nigga that came out of my balls." Devon hated that he admitted to Alex that he didn't want a child. It was even worse that she liked to throw shit in his face that he said to her while he was deep off in her pussy. Any bitch should have sense enough to know that a nigga will tell you anything when you fuckin' him right.

"Okay, I'm sorry. I really miss you and want to see you. I haven't had the chance to feel you inside of me in over a week. We need to make something happen and soon because I'm getting restless."

"Like I said, don't start that shit. I'll be there to see you soon. Don't reach out to me no more today," Devon sternly directed before ending the call without giving Alex a chance to respond.

"You okay?" Keyanna came prancing around the corner when Devon was about to put his phone back into his pocket. "Why do you look so upset?"

"I just got off the phone with one of my workers. They fucked up something on one of the houses we were building and now the homeowner isn't happy. I have to go smooth things over with them," he lied.

"Damn. I'm sorry to hear that. Go ahead and handle your business. I'm going to try to get a nap in while DJ is sleep," she told him.

Devon placed a sensual kiss on Keyanna's lips. She was so close up on him, that he knew she could feel his dick poking her.

"What you been thinking about?" Keyanna asked him, licking her lips.

"I just can't wait until your damn time up so I can get some. A nigga been hurting for some of that gushy shit."

"I know baby, and I'm sorry. Since I didn't have a regular delivery, I have to wait a little longer. You know what the doctor said when I had my C-section, so I have to wait eight weeks."

"Well, he came out of your stomach, not your mouth. Put that mufucka to work," Devon requested.

Devon didn't have to say another word. Keyanna instantaneously dropped to her knees and undid Devon's pants. His dick was so hard that it was pointing at her. Keyanna opened her mouth and took all nine of Devon's inches inside of it. She was sucking and slurping to the point that she began to gag. Devon loved when she gagged on his dick.

"Make that shit sloppy," he instructed her.

Keyanna pulled his dick out of her mouth and spit on it. She used one of her hands to rub the spit around before popping his dick back in her mouth. When Devon looked down, he noticed Keyanna was playing with herself. That turned him on even more. He closed his eyes and visualized actually being inside of her. He loved the wet and warm feeling he got whenever he entered her. Keyanna had a fat, juicy pussy, and he wanted so badly to be swimming inside of it.

"Ugghhhh... I can't wait to get that pussy again," he growled.

Keyanna started moaning with his dick in her mouth. That sent vibrations throughout his body, and he knew for a fact that he was about to explode. He looked back for something that could hold him up as his body began trembling. He back peddled toward the island where he rested his back to keep from falling and hitting the floor. Keyanna was sucking his dick as if her life depended on it. It was ten times better than the last time he could remember her sucking it.

"Fuck.... Your ass been practicing or some shit," he groaned loudly, right before all of his seeds were expelled down her throat. She looked up at him and licked her lips with a smile on her face. He could sense that meant she was happy with what she'd just done. She swallowed every last one of his seeds.

"Damn, girl. You trying to make sure you keep me happy, huh?" Devon spoke. That was the only thing he could think to say.

"Of course... Just like you won't leave room for another man to come in and take your place, I'm certainly not leaving room for another bitch to come in and take mine. Now, go clean yourself up and get ready for work. I plan on sucking your soul out tonight," Keyanna surprisingly spoke.

Devon wasn't used to her talking so freaky to him, but he was loving every moment of it and couldn't wait to get home later tonight. What bothered him was how Keyanna was doing everything she could to keep him happy in order to avoid another woman coming in between them, but another woman already did. How was he going to stop things before they got too far?

### Chapter Six:

Porscha could hear *Count on Me* by CeCe Winans and Whitney Houston playing on her phone. She ran to her room where she'd left her phone because she knew it was Keyanna calling her. That had been her ringtone ever since they declared themselves best friends, and Porscha had no intentions on changing it. She didn't give a damn how old the song was. Plus, anything of Whitney Houston's was a classic, and anybody that didn't like it could kiss her ass.

She was supposed to have a meeting with a potential client earlier this morning, but she pushed the meeting back because she was sleepy and didn't want to go into the meeting yawning and seeming unprofessional.

"Hello," she greeted Keyanna when she answered the phone.

"Bitccchhhhhh..." Keyanna sang through the phone. "What the fuck you doing?" Keyanna probed.

"Heyyyyy bestie! I'm just now waking back up. I have a lunch meeting with a potential client, and then I have to meet with one of the investors for my make-up line this evening. How are you and my God-baby doing?"

"We're doing great. I just wish DJ would learn to stay up during the day and sleep at night like a normal person does," Keyanna expressed, giggling.

"That's what babies do to you. I'm glad I don't have those problems," Porscha bragged.

"Shut up, bitch!" Keyanna commented, and they both laughed.

"I'm glad you called. I've been needing to talk to you. I just don't call you because I know you're busy with the baby, and I don't want to disturb you unless I have to."

"Don't ever not call me. We are best friends, and when you hurt, I hurt. What's going on with you?"

"I've been having these crazy ass dreams and they seem so real. It's almost as if something is about to happen and these dreams are my warning. Do you think I should go see one of those psychics to see what the dreams mean?"

"No, but maybe you should try going back and talking to your therapist. I remember the last time you had those dreams; the therapist was the only person that made you feel better about them," Keyanna suggested.

"That is true. But these dreams are totally different. Something is about to happen, and I don't know what it is. When I talk to Michael about them, he says that everything is good. But, I'm still iffy. You know what I'm saying?"

"I completely understand, sis. I'm sure they are nothing. If anything, maybe they are a sign of a blessing that may be heading your way."

While Porscha appreciated that Keyanna always tried to remain positive, she knew her thoughts would change if she knew exactly the kind of dreams that Porscha was having. She was too embarrassed by them to want to explain them to anyone other than her husband. She felt that if he told her they were good, then she needed to believe him. After all, they had bank accounts with millions of dollars in them and credit cards that had high limits on them. Not to mention, they owned their house and mostly all of their cars. So what the hell did she really have to worry about?

"Where's Devon?" Porscha changed the subject because she was tired of talking about her mental health issues.

"He's gone to work. I think he's a little bothered with me though," Keyanna admitted, which wasn't uncommon since they told each other everything.

"Why would he be bothered with you? I swear your relationship is relationship goals," Porscha exaggerated. She rolled her eyes since she knew that Keyanna couldn't see her.

"Because we just had DJ and so I can't have sex right now."

"Girl, don't nobody listen to that six week shit. You better start popping those damn birth control pills and give that man some. I wish the hell I would tell Michael he can't get none. That nigga would tackle me like he was a linebacker," Porscha joked. She wasn't about to tell Keyanna that she really didn't fuck Michael as often as she bragged about because she knew Keyanna was going to start questioning her about it. Everyone thought she had a picture-perfect marriage, and it was her intention to keep it that way.

"Now that's the relationship that's goals. You have your own business that you're working on, and Michael is doing his thang in the real estate world. You can't go anywhere without people knowing who one of y'all or both of y'all are," Keyanna commented, reminding Porscha of all the success her and Michael had been building for themselves.

"I guess you're right. I guess being go-getters did pay off for us. But, Devon has his own company, and you can practically go after any job you want, so don't downplay what y'all have," Porscha emphasized.

"Oh, I don't. I know that we are all beyond blessed and therefore, I have no reason to complain about anything. Anyways, I have to get off this phone. DJ is woke, and I know he's ready to eat." Porscha looked at the phone and wanted to make sure she wasn't tripping. Was Keyanna really getting off the phone with her because the baby was crying?

"Why you can't multi-task. You can feed him and talk to me at the same time?" Porscha was pretty much demanding Keyanna to stay on the phone with her. But when Keyanna laughed and hung the phone up anyways, Porscha felt some type of way. She tried calling Keyanna back, but when Keyanna didn't answer the phone, Porscha threw her phone across the room.

Porscha continued to get herself together for the client that she was going to meet. She'd had a love for makeup ever since she could remember. She'd researched a lot of the cosmetic lines to see what colors they didn't have or if there was something that their makeup couldn't do and was determined to create a makeup brand that would do it all. From mascara that would make your lashes look full and can be worn for three days without coming off, even when you sleep, to lipstick that changed according to your mood and the weather; Porscha was determined to have it all.

Being a certified makeup artist, Porscha made sure to stay up to date with what looked good, what colors popped together, how to fix your makeup in a way that your whole outfit would pop, and etc. She always would use her friends as guinea pigs, but to be moving up to having celebrity clients and doing whole wedding parties, Porscha was happy with her accomplishments.

After getting herself together, she gathered all of the samples and ideas she put together for the bride she was going to meet. She knew she'd done well enough in their previous meetings to get the bride to agree to allow her to do everyone's makeup for the wedding, but she still wanted to take her work to get the final go-ahead. Plus, she had a contract that she needed the bride to sign so she could go ahead and get her deposit.

Porscha locked up the house and got inside of her car that was parked in the garage. When she let the garage door up, she noticed that same white van parked across the street from their house. She felt like they were being watched, but she didn't understand what anybody would want to watch them for. She knew her and Michael were both legit in everything that they did. That made her wonder if someone was casing her house to rob it. That was the only explanation she could think of.

Curiosity got the best of her. She drove up next to the van and let her window down. The driver turned his head like he couldn't see her. Porscha was not one to be ignored. She got out of her car and tapped on the window.

"Why the hell am I doing this shit like this fool won't shoot me?" she asked herself as the man began letting the window down.

"Hey, how you doing?" he cheerfully asked. Porscha almost busted out laughing because the man sounded just like Wendy Williams to her.

"I'm fine, but what are you doing? I've noticed you out here a few times and I know you don't live over here. Do I need to call the police on you?" she questioned him, trying her best to look around him to see what was inside the van.

"No. I bring my brother over here to the woman that lives in this house." The man pointed to the house he was parked next to.

"Woman? There's no woman that lives in that house," Porscha strongly informed him.

"To my brother, that's his woman." The man winked at her. Porscha's face frowned up as she became disgusted. She figured the man was telling her that his brother was gay. She wasn't one to judge, so she decided to leave it alone. Then she went to thinking and had to say something else to the man.

"That man is married," Porscha explained.

"I know. That's why I don't park in the driveway. I park over here in case someone comes over uninvited. Then, my brother can sneak out the back and run over here, and we can speed away like nothing happened. Trust me, this has nothing to do with you or your house," the man assured her. But Porscha still didn't believe what he was saying.

"Yeah, okay," she told him and sauntered back over to her car.

Once Porscha had gotten back inside of her car, she looked over at the man and then at the house that he said his so-called brother had gone into. Porscha was very good with reading people and she knew that her neighbor was nowhere near gay. Since she knew the man was lying to her, she decided she was just going to have the bride come to her house. She didn't feel comfortable leaving it because she just knew the man was going to break into her house.

Porscha pulled back into her driveway and called the bride who agreed to come to her home before she called the alarm company and asked that they install cameras around their house. When the company agreed, she tried her best to get them to come the next day. While Porscha wasn't happy with that, she had no choice but to take it. She just told herself that she would not leave her house unattended for any given reason. She picked up her phone to call to get some of her other appointments rescheduled and the rest, she moved to her house before she went to prepare her office for her consultation.

### *Chapter Seven:*

Michael sat behind his oak L-shaped desk and waited for one of his meetings to start. His morning started off rocky because he was tired, but he was quickly able to bounce back from it. Ultimately, he knew that him being tired had nothing to do with his bad morning. It was the fact that Porscha tried to kill him, he practically had to beg Keyanna for help, and he felt like he was being watched.

"Mr. Alexander, your client is here for their meeting," Angelique told Michael over the intercom.

"Send him in," he told her as he waited for J-Dubb to enter his office. He stood from behind his desk and walked around to greet J-Dubb.

"Come on in and have a seat," he directed him. Michael then went over to the large file cabinet that was by his door. He removed his keys from his pocket to unlock the cabinet. Inside, he pulled out two large files and then went back around his desk to have a seat.

"How's my money looking?" J-Dubb inquired.

"Bro, your shit is looking real good. I've invested the money into having this subdivision built up. Of course, you're going to see the money going out before you see it come in. But in the end, your bank account is going to be fat as fuck," Michael explained.

One thing that Michael did that Porscha and no one else really knew was that he was using his real estate agency to clean money for some of the big time dope boys around Memphis. He would help them by having them buy houses, fixing them up, and selling them for damn near two times more than they paid for it. With his heavy hitters that gave him millions to clean, he'd help them invest in getting new subdivisions built and they'd sell those houses for double as well. When the IRS or Feds go to looking into the money, it would all come back clean.

Michael had been doing it for over three years, and he loved every minute of it. The adrenaline rush he got from doing something he knew was illegal and being able to get away with it gave him an indescribable feeling. Michael may have loved it, but he knew it was something he wouldn't be able to do forever. All good things come to an end, and he didn't want his end to be with him being scared to drop the damn soap.

"I'm glad everything is looking on the up and up. But, I got a potna' that I want you to meet. He in the game like me, and he trying to clean his money up too," J-Dubb informed Michael. Michael immediately went to thinking that something was up.

"What I tell you about bringing new people to me? I told you that once we finish off the last two transactions that I promised you, that I was done with this shit," Michael fussed. He thought he was putting his foot down. But J-Dubb went out of his way to convince him to stay in business with him just a little while longer.

"Damn, I know that. But you 'bout this money just like I am. You don't want your wife to know that this real estate shit is just a cover for your ass, and without our money, you'd be broke. I'm trying to help your punk ass out. Now, either you want to meet him, or you don't," J-Dubb quipped.

Michael began thinking about things. He had been lying to Porscha for a while about the amount of money that he really had. That was the only reason he promised to do two more transactions with J-Dubb. He knew it'd help cover some of the bills that he didn't pay because he fucked off the money. Then he thought that J-Dubb bringing him another deal may help him out enough to where he can get those millions he promised Porscha they had and not have to worry about working again.

"Well, what you gon' do because this him texting me now," J-Dubb told Michael. Michael stared at J-Dubb while he played on his phone. It was hard for him to say no because he needed the money desperately.

"Aight. I might meet with him, but it won't be today. I gotta wrap my mind around if this is going to be the right decision for me or not. I'll text you and let you know what I decide."

"Bet." J-Dubb stood up and gave Michael some dap. Michael walked over to the file cabinet and placed J-Dubb's file back in it and locked it before opening the door for J-Dubb to leave.

The rest of the day ran smoothly for Michael. He was elated when he got a text from Keyanna saying they would be there by the weekend. He wasn't going to tell Porscha anything. He was hoping that the surprise would get him back in her good graces. That still was not going to stop him from bringing up the fact that she tried to burn him with scalding hot water, again.

Before he left the office for the day, he decided he would give his mother a call. He normally liked to call and talk to her at least three times a week, but he hadn't called her none this week. From the way his mother was, it was no secret that she was going to give him hell as soon as he called her.

"What nigga?" Momma Rose answered the phone.

"Really, ma? Is that how you talk to your favorite child?"

"Let my favorite child call me, and we shall see," she snapped. She was not hiding the fact that she had an attitude with him at all.

"So, we doing that now?" he asked. He was becoming annoyed with her.

"Yep. Tell my favorite child to call me, and we shall see." With that being said, she hung up the phone on him.

"Bitch!" Michael hollered out. That was right before he dialed her number back.

"What nigga?"

"Again?"

"I don't care who call my phone. If I ain't fuckin' witcha, I just ain't fuckin' witcha," she explained.

"Why you always gotta exaggerate with shit?"

"Who said I was exaggerating? I'm telling you some real nigga shit. Now what do you want?" she asked. At least that time, she seemed a lot calmer to him.

"I was just calling to check on you. This has been a rough week for me, and whenever something is going on, I know I can count on you to be honest with me and make me feel better," he admitted to her.

"Son, I understand that. But you also need to be talking to your wife. You're her responsibility now. If you go to her like a man should and talk to her about what's bothering you, then you will be fine."

"She's the problem," Michael grunted.

"Oh, I knew it. I just wanted to hear you say it." His mother laughed and further irritated Michael.

"I have a client coming in. I'll call you back, Momma." He hung up the phone without giving it a second thought that he was being disrespectful.

"These women in my life are not about to run me crazy," he ranted. Michael grabbed all of his belongings and got up to leave the office. Angelique was still there when he was about to get on the elevator.

"Wait up, Michael." Angelique jumped up from behind her desk. There was no one in the waiting area, and that made Michael nervous. He'd never been inappropriate with Angelique, but she tried him all the time. "I was just thinking that we should play cops and robbers." She took one of her fingers and ran it down his chest.

"Cops and robbers, huh? And how do you suggest we do that?" he inquired, playing along with her.

"We can always start by you beating me with your nightstick." Without warning, she grabbed his dick.

"Oh..." He jumped back. "Are you trying to get both of us killed?"

"Killed by who?"

"By my damn wife. Porscha would bury both of our asses alive if I fucked around on her. Plus, I love my wife, so you need to back the fuck down," he cautioned her.

Michael turned and jogged toward the elevator. He made a mental note to talk to his partner when he returned to work about getting a new secretary. Angelique had become a big problem, and he didn't have time to deal with the shit. He'd rather lose her as a secretary than lose Porscha as a wife.

### *Chapter Eight:*

It had been a few days since Keyanna talked to Michael about making the trip to Memphis to visit them. She was actually excited about leaving Mississippi with the baby for the first time. She was really just anxious to see how he would do when they went on a long trip.

"You all packed?" Devon asked Keyanna while she was in the room changing the baby. He strolled inside the room and sat in the rocking chair next to the crib.

"Yes. I'm just making sure DJ is good before we get on the road. You got everything that you need?"

"Yes. I'm just waiting on you," Devon muttered. He seemed uninterested in the trip, Keyanna, and DJ. She looked at him and saw how his eyes lit up every time his phone went off, and she was determined to find out why.

"You okay over there?" she questioned.

"Yes, why you ask?"

"You all in that phone," she hissed.

"You know how Facebook is." Devon chuckled.

"No, I don't have Facebook," Keyanna replied. Devon and everyone else knew that Keyanna didn't do social media because she didn't like how it took over people's lives.

The doorbell rang while Devon and Keyanna was in the room with the baby.

"I'll get it," Devon told her and carelessly set his phone down on the changing table. Keyanna took that as her chance to go through it since it was unlocked.

As fast as she could, Keyanna scrolled through any texts that looked suspicious to her. She tried to go through his Facebook, but since she couldn't navigate the site, she didn't bother wasting any time.

"What the hell are you doing?" Devon asked Keyanna when he returned from answering the door.

"I was trying to Google a number," she lied.

"Where is your phone?" he probed. He was livid.

"It's in the room. What's the big deal with me using your phone to look up a number? I'm your wife." She walked up on him, daring him to say the wrong thing.

"The big deal is that your ass is looking through my damn texts like you don't trust me." She really wanted to tell him that she didn't, but she kept that comment to herself. She didn't want to say the wrong thing and risk him canceling the trip altogether.

"I was not. When I picked your phone up, you'd left it on your text. That's your fault, not mine."

Devon snatched his phone out of her hand. He looked her up and down like he wanted to hit her. Keyanna became nervous because she'd never seen that side of Devon before. He was always so kind and gentle with her; unless they were having sex.

"Don't fuckin' lie to me. You must think I'm some dumb nigga," he told her.

"No, I don't, and I'm not lying. This is what the phone was on when I picked it up," she argued.

"Keyanna, if I hit women, I'd knock your teeth down your throat. You over here trying to make it look like I'm cheating on your ass or some shit. And I know for a fact that my phone wasn't on this fuckin' message because it's damn July and the last texts in this conversation were sent way back in damn December."

Keyanna knew she was caught, but she wasn't going to give in that easy. For Devon to be so upset, he had to have been trying to hide something. An innocent person wouldn't dare trip out the way that he was. She picked the baby up just in case he got froggy enough to really try to hit her. Surely, he wouldn't be stupid enough to try anything while she had the baby in her arms.

"Apparently, you are doing something you don't have no business doing. We've been together for well over six years, and I've never had a reason to check your phone, so why the hell would I do it now? You've never even given me the reason to think that you were cheating," she told him, even though she knew she was lying. Keyanna loved Devon and knew he'd give her the world, but she felt like the changes she went through since being pregnant pushed him away. He didn't even look at her the way he used to. While she hadn't said anything to him or anyone else about it, that really bothered her.

"I'm not about to defend myself to bullshit. I have who I want, and she's standing in front of me, holding my seed. If I wanted to be anywhere else, then I'd be there."

"Then me picking up your phone shouldn't have been this big of a deal. That's unless you have something you want to tell me. Is there anything that you need to be telling me that I don't already know?" she questioned him.

"I'll tell you what... Don't ask no questions, and I won't tell you no lies," he replied to her before turning to walk out the room. The statement went over her head for a brief moment, but when she thought about what it meant, she laid the baby down in the crib and ran out the door behind him.

"What the fuck did you mean by that? You talking about don't ask you no questions and you won't have to tell me any lies. Devon, I will put my foot down your throat if you're cheating on me," she threatened him.

"I already told you that I'm with who I want to be with. Now if you keep going with all these fuckin' questions and being dramatic, then I'm going to call this whole trip off."

Keyanna was nowhere near done questioning Devon about what he'd just said to her. At the same time, she knew that if she kept going with the questions, he was truly going to call the trip off, and she didn't want that. She needed to get to Porscha to figure out what was going. Porscha was like Matlock. If there was anything that she needed to know, she'd find it within a blink of an eye. So if Devon was hiding something from her, Keyanna knew she could count on Porscha to get to the bottom of it.

"I'm sorry, baby. I was wrong for going through your phone. Can you forgive me?" she apologized in an attempt to get back on Devon's good side.

"You good, Key. I'm sorry I hollered at you. You didn't deserve that. But you need to trust me. I go to work every day so that you don't have to."

"I understand," she told him and pulled him in for a hug. He kissed her on the forehead and walked away from her.

Keyanna went back to the nursery and tended to DJ. She made sure he was dressed before grabbing him and his bag and walking out the door. She headed to the front door to put DJ's bags with the other suitcases. Then, she went to strap DJ into his car seat while Devon loaded up the car.

"Is that everything?" he asked her.

"I need to grab my purse, phone, and his milk, and I'll be ready," she informed him.

Devon stood outside their Ford Explorer while Keyanna ran back inside the house. She grabbed everything she needed and then walked through the house to make sure everything was off and that anything that needed to be unplugged, was. She set the alarm and pranced out the door back to the car. She was excited for her trip and couldn't wait to surprise her bestie.

### *Chapter Nine:*

Devon stood outside the house waiting on Keyanna to return. He used that time to go through his phone to delete anything that may have looked suspect in case Keyanna tried to go through his phone again. He opened up the private folder he had that was password protected and made sure any pictures or texts that he wanted to keep were safely in that folder.

"I'm ready," Keyanna sang when she locked the door and was walking back to the car.

Devon didn't respond to her. He got inside the SUV and crank it up while he waited for Keyanna to get in the back seat with DJ. Devon glanced up in the rearview mirror and noticed that Keyanna had put her sunglasses on. Anytime she did that, he knew she was upset about something and that he was going to have to give her time to cool down before speaking with her.

The first hour and a half of the trip was silent. Devon let his window down a little so that the sound of the wind blowing could soothe him. His nerves were on a thousand because he didn't like Keyanna being mad at him. He wondered if she saw something in his phone that would imply he was talking to another woman and just hadn't told him about it yet. He loved her and didn't want to lose her. But at the same time, there was something else that he needed that she just wasn't giving him at the moment.

"Can you pullover so I can change the baby and we can get something to eat?" Keyanna finally spoke to him.

"Sure. What do you have a taste for? That'll let me know which exit I need to get off on," he replied.

"Anything but McDonald's. That shit's disgusting," she commented.

Devon passed a few exits before he came to one that had a McAllister's. He knew that Keyanna loved their broccoli spuds, so he was going to get her one as a peace offering.

"It's lunch time, so let's go sit down and eat. That's something we haven't been able to do in a while," he told her. Keyanna smiled and nodded her head in agreement with him. He felt for a moment that everything was going to be okay.

When Devon got to the restaurant, it was packed. Because of where it was located in Grenada, he didn't think there would be so many people there. He felt himself getting antsy because he was never someone that liked to be around a lot of people. When Keyanna reached over and touched his shoulder, he felt a whole lot better. That was something that only she had the capability to do to him.

"I'm going to go in to use the bathroom and take care of DJ. Can you go ahead and order the food?"

"Yeah, take your time. I'm not going anywhere," he told her. Devon winked at her and made her blush. That was the

Keyanna he fell in love with. He wished it was like that all the time.

Devon went to the counter and ordered their food as Keyanna requested and then went to find them somewhere to sit in the crowded restaurant. For some reason, it seemed like all eyes were on Devon. He surveyed his surroundings to see if there were people staring at him and there weren't. He was paranoid, and he knew it was because of what he was doing behind Keyanna's back. His heart beat sped up and his breathing became erratic as he thought of how close he was to being caught cheating. He didn't know what he'd do if Keyanna walked away from him and took DJ with her. True enough, he wished he didn't have a child because they didn't have the freedom that they had before DJ's arrival and because Keyanna wasn't the carefree and spontaneous woman that she used to be. But, he'd somewhat gotten used to the idea of him being there.

Devon continued to observe the sitting area of the restaurant when his eyes landed on a young white woman he'd caught staring at him. When they made eye contact, she licked her lips and smiled at him. Devon's dick starting to rise in his pants. White women weren't his preference, but he was so sex deprived, he'd give her a run for her money. The woman waved at him, and he waved back just as Keyanna walked out of the bathroom carrying a fussy DJ.

"What's wrong with him?" Devon asked when Keyanna made it over to him. She tried to hand him DJ, but Devon pushed him away.

"Can you please hold your son?" Keyanna loudly said to him. Devon was so embarrassed that he roughly grabbed DJ out of her hands. "The fuck! I know you were not just rough with him," Keyanna scoffed, yanking DJ back from him.

"Why are you making a scene? You're the one that just jerked him away from me," Devon argued. He didn't like the way Keyanna was showing her natural black ass for no reason.

"Why are you? Do you see how you just yanked him out of my hands? He's just a baby. You have to be gentle with him."

"You telling me to be gentle with him, but again, your ass just jerked him away from me. If you ask me then your ass was rougher than I was."

"Well, I wasn't asking you shit. I was telling you that you were rough, and I didn't like it. The way I took him back was just a mother's natural response," Keyanna pleaded her case. Devon realized that Keyanna was right and had every reason to be mad at him.

"I'm sorry. I didn't notice that I was handling him so poorly. Can you please sit down so we can enjoy lunch? I don't want to fight any longer," Devon honestly told her. Keyanna softened up a bit and sat down so that she could get DJ quiet.

Devon watched as Keyanna coddled DJ so well. He admired how she was so patient and loving with him. He almost hated that he really hadn't bonded with his son when DJ was the only child he knew that he'd ever have. He'd made an appointment to get a vasectomy without Keyanna knowing. He was getting it done as soon as they got back from Memphis. To him, that was perfect timing since Keyanna was still not able to have sex, so that would give him enough time to recover after the surgery.

"Maybe we should just get the food to go," Keyanna suggested.

"Are you sure? We only have a little over an hour left to drive before we get to Memphis. I kinda wanted to spend a little time with you. You really haven't gotten out of the house much since DJ has been born," Devon asserted.

"Yeah, but if this woman don't quit staring at you like you're a piece of chicken, I'ma give her this five piece," Keyanna advised him. Devon couldn't do anything but laugh.

"Sit your feisty ass down. You know I don't like white meat," he assured her. Keyanna gave the woman a hard eye roll before she turned around to feed DJ.

Devon shook his head at the woman. That was his way of telling her that Keyanna wasn't somebody she wanted to try because although she carried the look of a geek, her geek was gangsta.

The food came out as Keyanna finished feeding and burping DJ. She carefully placed him in his car seat so that she could eat.

"This looks good," she happily said before she started eating. Devon laughed because Keyanna never ate without praying first. "What's so funny?" She glanced up at him with a piece of broccoli hanging out the side of her mouth.

"You know you didn't pray, right?"

"Yeah, I did. When that woman kept looking at you, I prayed that God gave me the strength to keep my hands, feet, and other objects to myself. I also prayed that we could eat our food in peace," she informed him. Keyanna did a half smile and went back to enjoying her food. The only thing Devon could do was shrug his shoulders.

Their mealtime was great. They had a great conversation and made a few plans for some things they wanted to do when they got to Memphis.

"I love you, D," Keyanna told him out of nowhere.

"I love you, too, Key," he replied.

"I'm thinking about ignoring these next few weeks. It's been a while since I had DJ, and I don't hurt as much as I was initially, so you know what that means..."

Devon's head shot up, and he dropped the food that was on his fork onto his lap. He knew what Keyanna was getting at and that wasn't good for him. Some kind of way, he had to persuade her to stick with what the doctor said, or he was going to be fucked out of getting his vasectomy.

### Chapter Ten:

Michael was on his way out of his office when he was approached by a big, burly man. His senses told him that something wasn't right, so he fought with the latch on his briefcase, trying to get it opened. Because of the type of work he did, he always made sure he was packing. He had a 9 mm Taurus that he was trying to get to. The man walked up on him and stuck something sharp into Michael's side.

"You can stop moving and do what I say, or I'll kill you right where you stand," the man told him.

Immediately, Michael stopped moving. There was no way he'd be able to get to his gun in enough time to defend himself. A sharp pain spread through his body as the object pierced further into his side. He didn't know what was going on, but he prayed that he'd be able to make it out alive.

"What do you want from me?" Michael questioned the man.

"Shut up and do as I say," the man retorted. Michael snapped his mouth shut and nodded his head in understanding. "Let's go back up to your office so we can have a talk. Don't try to alert anybody of what's going on or Porscha is dead," the man warned him.

"What? Where's my wife? I want to talk to her," Michael demanded.

"You are not in a position to be issuing out demands. Porscha is doing fine... for now," the man replied. He let out an evil chuckle that sent sputters down Michael's spine. He felt the hair on the back of his neck stand up in fear of what could possibly happen.

Michael followed the man's instructions and marched him back up to his office. It was the end of the day, so there was barely anyone else around. Angelique was getting on the elevator as Michael was getting off. He heard her say something to him, but he kept walking because he didn't want to put her in any danger. Not only that, but she'd been bitter ever since he talked to his partner about possibly letting her go. He kept a distance from her because something told him it would be a matter of time before she tried to get back at him.

"You did good," the man told him. Michael looked down and could see the blood dripping from his shirt. "Have a seat," the man directed. Michael sat in the chair that was positioned in front of his desk while the man walked around and sat behind the desk. "I could get used to this," the man joked.

"What do you want from me?" Michael asked again, wanting to know what was going on.

"I hear you spoke to my dear friend, J-Dubb. He told me what kind of business you were in, and I need your help. The Feds have been watching me hard, so I need to clean my money up."

"What are you telling me for?" Michael stupidly asked. As soon as the man mentioned the Feds, Michael was ready to tell him hell no. He was not about to put his neck on the line any more than he had already been doing. He couldn't risk going to jail, losing his career, rupturing both his and Porscha's reputation, or losing Porscha.

"Don't be funny, nigga. You know exactly why I'm telling you. I heard you were the man for the job." Michael smirked a little when he heard that because he liked the idea of people knowing how good he was at what he did. What he didn't like was the fact that he was being threatened to go into business with someone that he didn't know and didn't care to know.

"Look, I appreciate the compliment and all, but I told J-Dubb that I was getting out of the business, so I don't know why he would send you here."

"You can get out of the business once you help me," the man chided. His fist was clenched, and he appeared to be ready to knock the fuck out of Michael if he said the wrong thing. Michael wasn't scared of no man, but the fact that the nigga had someone else with him told Michael that he came there on a mission.

"If you have the Feds on your ass and I help you, that means they are going to be on my ass too. I have too much to lose, so I can't help you. Sorry," Michael apologized and stood up from his chair.

"Sit your five-dollar ass down before I make change," the man barked. Michael hurriedly sat back down. He knew the man had a knife, and if he were able to get to his gun, he'd be able to take him. What he didn't know was if the man had a gun as well. Chances are, he did, and by the time Michael could've gotten his gun out of his briefcase, the man would've been able to decorate his body with bullet holes. That was a risk that Michael was not willing to take.

"I can't help you. I can refer you to someone else."

"I don't want someone else. I want you. Truthfully, you don't have a choice. You see this..." the man pulled out his phone and showed Michael a few pictures of Porscha.

"Where is she?" Michael bellowed. He was furious that the man could do something to Porscha. He loved her and would rather die than to see anything happen to her.

"She's safe...for now. As long as you do what I need you to do, then everything will be fine." The man had a sincere expression on his face, but Michael still didn't trust the shit.

"How much money is it?" He wondered exactly how much money the man needed him to clean. He figured that if he could do it in as little as a few months, then he'd be fine. But, he was still worried about the fact that the Feds were involved. As soon as Michael touched the money, his world could come crashing down.

"Let's just say it's going to take you a while to get it clean," the man told Michael. Michael shook his head. If he would've known that getting involved with drug dealers from the jump would land him in the type of shit that he was currently in, then he wouldn't have ever started it. His partner Jared is who got him started with it, and he was determined to find a way out.

"I'll help you maybe two or three times, and after that, I'm done. You're going to have to find another way to take care of your business," Michael harshly dictated.

"Well, you better know how to clean a lot of money within those two or three times or you're going to be working for me a lot longer than you think." The man stood to leave out of the office.

"Wait... What is your name? How do I contact you?" Michael probed. He wanted to find out as much as he could about the man so that he could do a little research of his own.

"You can call me Deuce, and don't worry about contacting me. I'll contact you when the time is right," Deuce claimed and walked on out the door.

Michael jumped up and ran to the bathroom. His nerves were so bad, he was shakin' like a hoe in church. The rightful thing for him to do was to call Porscha to make sure she was okay, but he wanted to check his bruise first. He lifted his shirt up and saw the small niche that was in his skin.

"Muthafucka," he said aloud. Grabbing some paper towels, he wet them in an attempt to wash away the blood. He grabbed a few dry ones and stuck them to his skin. They'd have to work until he was able to get home and bandage himself up.

Michael decided he was going to just go home and not call Porscha. He didn't want to upset her by being panicky on the phone. He was so worried about her that he ran out of the office without locking everything up or grabbing his briefcase.

### Chapter Eleven:

Porscha had just finished a Skype call with a bride that lived in Nashville. She said she heard about Porscha's work and wanted to know if she would be willing to drive to Nashville on the day of her wedding to do the whole bridal party. Not being one to turn down any money, Porscha happily agreed. Plus, it would give her an excuse to get out of Memphis for a while.

She was about to head upstairs and get a nap in before her next meeting when the doorbell rang. She wasn't expecting any company, so she opened up her Vivint app on her phone to see if she could tell who it was from the cameras she had installed around the house. The moment she saw who it was, she jumped up and hightailed it to the door.

"Bestieeeeeee..." she yelled when she opened the door. "Why didn't you tell me that you were coming to visit?" she asked Keyanna, pulling her in for a big bear hug.

"Michael wanted to surprise you," Keyanna replied, trying to loosen Porscha's grip some. "Damn, you trying to choke me to death?" Keyanna commented.

"No, but I've missed you so much. We've never gone this long without seeing each other," Porscha reminded her.

"I know, but you know when you have a baby, life changes," Keyanna acknowledged.

Porscha dropped her head before replying, "I know."

"You gonna stand there talking all day or you gonna help me get some of the stuff out the car?" Devon called from behind Keyanna.

"Oh, I see you brought the seed of Chucky with you," Porscha snarled as if she was disgusted.

"Shut up, girl! You knew I wasn't getting on the road by myself, and I certainly wasn't going to leave my little one behind."

"You brought the baby? Where is he?" Porscha asked with a voice full of excitement. She damn near ran Keyanna over trying to get to the SUV to see the baby.

"Well, damn bitch!" Keyanna yelled out to her.

"My bad. I'm ready to lay eyes on my Godson."

"Hey to you, too, Porscha," Devon spoke when Porscha made it out to him.

"Sup?" Porscha responded and went straight for the car seat. She was in love the moment she laid eyes on DJ. "He's sooooo adorable; I want him," Porscha babbled as she admired how handsome DJ was.

"Sorry, sis, but you got to get your own," Keyanna teased. Whether she knew it or not, her comment stung Porscha. She'd been holding a secret from everyone that she swore was going to the grave with her.

Devon grabbed all the bags out of the car while Porsche helped Keyanna get DJ inside the house. Once everyone had gotten in the house, Keyanna laid DJ down in the basinet that Devon already had set up and joined Porscha in the living room.

"You don't know how much I've missed you," Porscha confessed to Keyanna.

"Yes, I do, because I've missed you too. What happened to us? We used to be so close," Keyanna pondered.

"We're still close; we're just in different places in life. You have your working man and baby, and I have my working man and I'm still trying to establish my career."

"How's that going? What all have you done so far?"

"Oh, that's right. I haven't had a chance to update you on what I've been doing. Girl, I've found so many new colors that I work with, and I've built up a clientele so big that I can't keep up with them. Sometimes, I feel like I've got too much going on, but I love every moment of it. I've been selling my makeup online, but I'm also working on my own store. I really want to work with celebrities," Porscha rambled while Keyanna sat there taking it all in.

"It'll happen. Just don't ever give up on what you want. Remember that nobody can stop you from reaching your goals but you."

"Thanks, sis. See, I'm so glad you're here. I needed to hear that."

"Bitch, I could've told you that shit over the phone," Keyanna teased.

"Yeah, you could've. But it's not the same as saying it face-to-face, bitch," Porscha replied, punching Keyanna in the arm playfully.

"Whatever. Now, are you going to show me around or what?"

"Haven't you been to this house?"

"Now you know damn well that I haven't been to this house. You were living in that house out in Collierville the last time we came up here."

"Damn, you're right. Come on here," Porscha insisted and practically jumped up from where she was sitting.

Porscha took Keyanna through the entire house, telling her a story about the reason she decorated each room the way that she did. When they stopped at the guest room that Porscha designated for them to stay in, Keyanna walked over and checked on the baby.

"Does he always sleep this peaceful?" Porscha asked.

"Yes, when he's sleep. I'm just ready for him to learn that the day is when you need to be up, and the night is when you need to sleep." Keyanna giggled, glancing down at DJ. "Seriously, he's the bright spot of my days. Then, the love that you have when you're a mother is different than any other love you'll ever experience." Porscha smiled at Keyanna as she rambled on and on about motherhood. She was really in her feelings a little bit, but she wasn't going to say anything because she didn't want to ruin Keyanna's happiness. "Oh, I'm sorry, sis." Keyanna turned and looked at Porscha.

"Sorry for what?" Porscha questioned, playing dumb.

"I'm going on and on about motherhood without thinking about your feelings. How have you been since the miscarriage?"

"Couldn't be better."

"Come on, Porscha. I know you. I can tel—" Keyanna was cut off by Porscha.

"If you know me, then you'd know that I don't want to talk about the shit. It wasn't my time, but it'll happen when it happens. No rush. Now, keep talking. I only want to talk about positive shit," Porscha snapped. She didn't want to be anybody's charity case or have them pitying her. She kept her hurt to herself because to her, that was how a real bitch operated.

"You have a great house, sis. I absolutely love ho—"

"That's great, boo," Porscha cut Keyanna off, again. "You want to go sit in the living room and have a talk? We need to catch up." Keyanna peered over at her like she wanted to say something, but she waited a moment before she began to speak again.

"I'll be here for a while, so we'll have plenty of time to catch up. Let me get a nap in while DJ is sleep, and I'll be as good as new." Keyanna yawned.

"Okay." Porscha had no choice but to understand, although she was a little sad that Keyanna couldn't focus on her right then.

Porscha figured she was drained from not only the trip, but because of how hot it was outside, so she didn't put up a fuss. She didn't know exactly how long they'd be staying, but she figured she'd have more than enough time to catch up with her bestie. She started planning out all the things she felt they'd be able to do while Keyanna was there, including going to Beale Street.

Porscha found herself in the living room, sitting on the couch in a daze. There were so many things running through her mind, and she felt the need to keep all of those thoughts to herself. She just didn't want to be judged by anyone. Keyanna was her best friend, true enough. But, Porscha was sure that she wouldn't understand what she was going through.

"Where's jackass?" Devon came from around the corner and joined Porscha in the living room.

"I'm looking at him," Porscha snidely commented. "Couldn't Keyanna have come by herself? You make my skin crawl."

"Yeah, I'm sure I do make it crawl. Just like you make me want to vomit up all of my food when I see that fugly ass face of yours."

"Good. Throw it up then. Maybe you'll lose enough body fluids to die from dehydration." Porscha let out a slight laugh as she stood from the couch.

"Ha-ha... You not funny."

"You seem to think so," Porscha implied and walked up on Devon.

"Don't start no shit, Porscha," Devon cautioned her.

"You started it the minute you stepped inside of my house. Now, I don't know how Keyanna runs your house back in Mississippi. But up here, whatever I want, I get!" she emphasized.

Devon leaned his head down and glared into Porscha's eyes. To her, it was as if his eyes were piercing inside of hers and getting a glimpse of her soul.

"And what is it that you want?" Devon asked.

Porscha cut her eyes to the side because there was just something about Devon that she couldn't put her finger on. It was like he could read her, and she didn't like that. Keyanna and Michael were the two people that should've been the closest to Porscha, but they weren't. She really thought Devon knew her better than anyone else. He moved his head forward and was about to kiss her until the front door flew open and Michael came trampling in. Porscha jumped back right as Michael paused. He turned his head to the side and looked between Porscha and Devon. Porscha didn't know how much he saw, but she prayed it wasn't enough for him to realize she'd been fuckin' her best friend's husband.

### Chapter Twelve:

"What the hell is going on?" Michael asked. He turned away from them and went toward the window. He looked out of the curtains to see if there was anyone out there. Because of the pictures that Deuce had of Porscha, he knew that he had to have been following them or had someone else doing his dirty work. That was when he thought about the white van that they'd seen parked across from their house on several occasions.

"Michael, why'd you come busting in the house like you're crazy?" Porscha asked him. She put her hand on his shoulder, and he jumped back. "Why are you so spooked?" Porscha continued to question him.

"It's nothing. I had a long day, so I'm trippin'. How was your day, baby?" Michael lied because he didn't want to worry Porscha. Not when he figured he had everything under control. Certainly, not in front of Devon.

Michael gave Porscha a kiss on the cheek before making eye contact with Devon. Porscha gave Michael a hug and thanked him for having Keyanna and Devon come up to surprise her before she left out of the room to give the men a chance to talk. For the longest time, there was nothing but silence in the room. Devon must've gotten tired of standing and decided to have a seat. He sat back on the couch and propped his feet up on the coffee table. Devon then grabbed the remote and turned the television on. He browsed through the channels for something to watch as if Michael wasn't standing there.

After some time, Michael couldn't take it anymore. He was over Devon, and they hadn't even made it through the first day. He wanted to help his wife by calling her best friend to visit, but he hoped that Devon wouldn't show his ass.

"Nigga, you got me fucked up." Michael marched over to the table and knocked Devon's feet on the floor. Devon jumped up like he was ready to go to war. Michael stood in his fight stance to show Devon that he was ready for whatever. Michael really wasn't the type to fight, but he didn't tolerate disrespect, and he didn't back down from anyone. Even if he felt that he'd lose, there was no way he was going to allow Devon to punk him in his own home.

"What's your mufuckin' problem?" Devon roared. "Don't put your gotdamn hands on me if I didn't touch you."

"This my damn house. You propped all up on my shit and flickin' my fuckin' channels like you pay bills in this bitch," Michael hissed.

"Why do we have to go through this shit every time we get together? Obviously, I intimidate yo' bitch ass," Devon scoffed.

"There is nothing about you that would intimidate me, and you surely don't have shit that I want. You own a house, and so do I. You have more than one car, and so do I; mine are fancier. Your wife stays at home while mine beats the streets every day on a hustle. You got money in the bank, and so do I; which I'm sure that my bank account is a tad bit fatter. Like I told yo' bitch ass, you don't have shit that I want," Michael boasted.

"The only reason a person brags about what they have is because they really don't have what they say they have, or their life isn't what it seems. For you, I'm going to go with the latter. I have absolutely everything you want and then some. You can put up your little front for your wife and your little minions, but I see straight through all your little bullshit."

"What bullshit is that?"

"The bullshit where you came running in here because I'm sure somebody scared your punk ass. What? Did they threaten to expose you for the fake you really are?"

"I'm sick of yo' mufuckin' ass, nigga. Get yo' shit and get out of my mufuckin' house. Ain't shit here for you."

"As long as my wife and seed are in this bitch, then I'll be in this bitch too," Devon snarled. "You got me all the way fucked up if you think that I'm going to leave my family here with your good for nothing ass."

"Oh, okay. You not gonna leave? I got you. Stay right there," Michael grumbled and stormed out of the room. A few seconds later, he returned with a small revolver. Devon looked at the gun and laughed.

"Didn't yo' daddy teach you not to bring out a gun unless you plan on using it?" Devon showed no fear as Michael held the gun on him.

Michael opened his mouth to speak right as Devon charged at him. As soon as Devon made contact with Michael, his hand slipped on the trigger and the gun went off. Porscha came dashing into the living room to see what was going on. Not long after Porscha got in there, Keyanna came running with the baby yelling for everyone to get down. Porscha was on the floor with the men as they tussled with one another. The gun fell to the side and made a loud thud.

"Stop it! Stop it, now!" Keyanna didn't bother trying to break up the fight. It had a lot to do with the fact that she was holding the baby in her arms.

The men stayed on the floor fighting, hitting Porscha a few times. It was evident that Porscha was pissed from being hit because she started swinging on both of the men. The only thing that broke the fight up was the sound of police sirens nearing the house.

"Oh, hell naw; somebody called the police. I'm not going to jail for no damn body," Keyanna barked and left out of the living room. Porscha felt the tears rolling down her cheeks and turned to face both men.

"One of you sons of bitches hit me. I don't know who it was, but you'd better know that I'm fuckin' pissed. This was some dumb shit that could've been avoided if you two would've acted like adults and not two fuckin' baboons!" Porscha bellowed. She was furious.

Michael picked up his gun and went to put it away. He went back into the living room to look at the damage that they'd caused. The coffee table was broken, and they'd managed to knock Porscha's favorite flower vase over and break it. Not to mention the damn hole in the ceiling from when the gun went off. Michael was pissed at his behavior but even more pissed that he allowed someone like Devon to push him over the edge.

**Knock... Knock...**

Michael already knew who it was knocking on the door, so he rushed to the door to try to shoo them away while Devon was in the living room trying to prop the table back up to avoid anything looking out of place.

"Hello, officers," Michael greeted them when he opened the door.

"Are you the homeowner?" one of the officers asked.

"Yes, how may I help you?"

"One of the neighbors called and said they heard a gunshot in the area, but they weren't sure where it came from. Did you hear anything?"

"No, nothing out of the ordinary. We are in Memphis; you know there is a gunshot heard every few seconds," Michael joked, but neither officer laughed.

"Are you home alone?"

"No, my wife is here along with her best friend, her husband and their little baby. Unless you know a newborn that can shoot a gun, I can assure you that there was no shooting coming from here," Michael replied. The officer attempted to look around Michael, but Michael had done an excellent job with blocking his view.

"Okay, well if you hear anything, please be sure to give us a call. Y'all have a good evening," the officer spoke and walked away. Michael expelled a loud sigh when he thought of how close he was to getting in trouble with the police. He worked too hard to end up losing everything he had because of Devon.

"If you so big and bad like you claim, why didn't you let 5-0 know that you were the one that let off the shot?" Devon asked.

"Fuck you, Devon!" Michael roared.

"Naw, you need to be fuckin' your wife. Maybe then she'd have some act right," Devon clapped back. Michael debated on saying something back to him, but he didn't need to engage in Devon's pettiness because it would only lead to another fight.

Michael shut the door and locked it. He knew that Keyanna and Porscha were both upset, but Porscha was his number one priority, so he made it a point to go check on her first. That was after he went to the kitchen to get something to put on his head.

### *Chapter Thirteen:*

"I can't believe this shit. Never have I ever had the police come to my house. What the hell were you thinking?" Porscha hollered at Michael who'd came in the room and sat on the foot of their bed with an ice pack on his head.

"I'm sorry, but you know damn well that I would never let a nigga come in my house and disrespect me. If a woman would've done that shit to you, how would you have handled it?"

"I wouldn't have gotten a fuckin' gun. You could've gone to jail, then what?"

"Why the hell would I end up in jail when I'm protecting my damn home? That nigga attacked me. Had he never touched me, the gun never would've gone off." Michael defended himself against his wife. She was the one person he should never have to worry about ever defending himself against. "Whose fuckin' side are you on?"

"It's not about being on anyone's side. You were both wrong, and as soon as I get the chance, I'm going to tell him the same damn thing," Porscha assured him.

"No, what you need to do is tell his ass to get out of my mufuckin' house. I thought I was doing the right thing by having Keyanna come visit you since you had been having those bad dreams, but apparently, I was wrong. I should've left their asses where they were."

"I'm not telling my best friend to leave." Porscha refused.

"Devon is not sleeping under my roof. This is my mufuckin' house; I'm the king of this castle, and I will not be uncomfortable where I lay my head. Now, either you can tell him to leave or I will."

"Michael, no. If he leaves then he's going to take Keyanna with him."

"I never said she had to leave, but he does. If she's not happy with my decision, then she can go and take that little baldheaded as baby with them. And if you don't like it, you can skedaddle your ass out the door right behind them," Michael scolded.

"Hol' the fuck up." Porscha jogged inside of their walk-in closet. Quickly, she changed her shoes and jogged back out the closet. She took the scrunchy that was on her wrist off and wrapped it around her hair. She faced Michael and engaged in an intense stare off with him. "Nigga, you got me all the way fucked up if you think you're going to put me out of my house. You can get your shit and get your mufuckin' ass out," Porscha snapped.

"Get the fuck on, Porscha. You coming out here like you Rambo. You might as well let your damn hair back down because you not about to move sh—" Michael didn't get to finish his statement before Porscha punched him in the nose.

Blood instantly started dripping from his nose, as Michael grabbed it in disbelief.

Porscha was shocked at her actions. Never had she and Michael gotten physical with one another outside of playfully wrestling with each other or having sex. She didn't know what it would mean for their relationship, but she knew that there were going to be some changes. As her thoughts ran rampant through her mind, she never let her guard down. She didn't know how Michael was going to react to her hitting him.

"Stupid bitch!" he barked. Porscha looked at him like he'd lost his mind.

"The fuck? Did you really just call me a bitch?"

"I called you what you're acting like; a ratchet ass bitch. Porscha, get the fuck out! I want you out of my house now," Michael roared.

Porscha stood frozen for a moment. When she gathered her thoughts and realized what was going on, she went back inside the closet. She grabbed the first suitcase that she could and started throwing shit in it. She didn't care what she grabbed or how she put it in the suitcase. By the time she was done, she was completely out of breath. Her chest heaved up and down as she tried to regain control of her breathing. Dragging the suitcase out of the closet, she dropped it in front of Michael.

"What's this?" he probed.

"Yo' shit," she replied.

"What the fuck you mean, my shit?"

"Exactly what the fuck I said. This is yo' shit. You can take your ass out the front door, or I can help you out of the window," Porscha advised him. Whether Michael wanted to believe it or not, Porscha was being as serious as a heart attack with him.

"I'm not leaving my house," Michael fumed.

"Oh, yes the fuck you are. I gave you two nice options on leaving. Now, I'm giving you a third option."

"And what's that?"

"I can take my black ass out the door and tell those officers the truth about the gun shot. I'm sure they won't have a problem helping you leave," she threatened him.

"Fuck this shit," Michael quipped. "I'm going to leave the house for a few hours, and when I get back, you better not be on that same bullshit," Michael commented and exited the room.

Porscha heard Keyanna and Devon hollering at each other from down the hall. If she would've known that this visit would've turned out the way that it did, she would've suggested that they went to a hotel before Michael even made it home.

Slamming her room door, she stormed inside the bathroom and sat on the toilet. Tears welled up in her eyes and fell before she knew it. She glanced up in the mirror and suddenly didn't recognize herself. She was displaying a side of herself that scared her. First, she tried to burn Michael with hot water. Then, she punched him in the face. Now, she had put him out. What was going on with her? She didn't know, but whatever it was, she knew she was going to have to get a handle on it and fast.

### *Chapter Fourteen:*

"I can't believe you would come up here and get into a fight with Michael like that. It's ridiculous. Why couldn't you act like a man? I've told you time and time again that you needed to be the bigger person," Keyanna scolded Devon. He looked out the window, not paying her any attention. "Don't you hear me talking to you?"

"I hear you fussing, but you must be talking to DJ because my mother ain't here," Devon responded.

"Fine. Don't listen," Keyanna squealed. Devon knew that meant she was about to cry. He hated the way he was acting with her, but he didn't think he was at fault for what happened.

"Don't cry, Keyanna. I'm sorry if I hurt you, but Michael started this shit," he called himself explaining.

"All you can say is that Michael started the shit? Really? You're such a fuckin' child. Grow the fuck up, Devon," Keyanna aggressively spoke. Devon stood there not knowing what to say.

Keyanna picked up DJ who had been lying in the basinet crying. She grabbed his diaper bag and the car keys. She made sure that Devon knew she was disgusted with his actions.

"Don't wait up for us," she told him and left out of the room. Devon ran out behind her. She wasn't supposed to be driving, and he didn't like the fact that she was willing to drive around Memphis and didn't know shit about the city.

"Where are you going?"

"Don't worry about it. I can handle myself."

"I know that you can't seriously be that mad at me. I was only defending myself. Why would you think I would let that nigga put his hands on me and not do anything about it?"

"Like I told you before, grow the fuck up," she spat. Keyanna locked DJ down in his car seat and jumped in the driver's seat. Devon stood by the SUV trying to reason with her, but there was no use. She had her mind made up. She wanted to be as far away from him as possible. He watched as she threw the car in drive and pulled away from the house.

Devon remained in the same spot until the vehicle was no longer in sight. He threw his hands in the air as if he were defeated and went back inside the home. Nobody was there but him and Porscha. He needed a way to go after Keyanna, but he didn't want to cause any tension between him and Porscha.

***Knock... Knock...***

He knocked on Porscha's bedroom door. He waited for a while before he ended up knocking again because his first knocks were unanswered.

"I know you're in there," he called out to her.

"So, what if the fuck I am?" Porscha snapped at him.

Devon pushed the door open and surveyed the disastrous room. Porscha had clothes scattered everywhere. There was even some broken glass on the floor. He saw where there was a brush near the mirror and took it as she used the brush to take her anger out on the mirror. Porscha was sitting on the bed with her back turned toward the door.

"Look, I'm sorry," he apologized to her.

"Are you really?" At this point, Porscha had turned to face Devon.

"Yes, I didn't mean for shit to go down the way that it did. We just got here. Whoever would've thought that shit would've gone so bad so quickly?"

"Why the hell can't the two of you just get along?" Porscha questioned him between sniffles.

"He don't like me. I mean, I guess I can see why, but damn," Devon replied.

"Why? I don't see why, so why don't you enlighten me on it."

"Be real with yourself, Porscha. You know just like I do that Michael is jealous of me. I have more than he ever did, and that includes you."

"He doesn't know that. Nobody knows what we have together." Porscha stood from the bed and gazed into Devon's eyes. "Do you think he suspects something?" she asked him.

"He has to. I mean, look at the way you look at me. You don't try to hide the fact that you have feelings for me."

"Yes, I do. I don't ever show anybody the way I truly feel about you," she replied to him.

"No, you don't. But why don't you show me? You tell me all the time that you love me, but you've never shown me exactly how much," Devon announced.

"I've shown you on more than one occasion how much I love you. Remember when I got that abortion because you didn't want any kids? That was real fucked up considering you told me you didn't want kids but turned right back around within the next two months and got my best friend pregnant."

"She's my fuckin' wife. What the fuck would I look like asking her to abort my seed?"

"She's your wife, but I'm the one that you're supposed to be in love with. I could've had my baby."

"I was not about to let that punk ass nigga raise my seed. I'm sorry, but that was never an option. What kind of man do you take me as?"

"One that only gives a damn about himself. That baby that she has doesn't even look like you. How do you know that he's even your son?"

"Because I branded that pussy. Keyanna isn't a hoe; she would never cheat on me," Devon fussed. He was furious that Porscha would even try to give him the idea that Keyanna stepped out on him. They both were fully aware of the type of person that Keyanna was, and a cheater was not a character trait of hers.

"She's not a hoe, but I am?"

"If the show fits..."

"Fuck you, Devon. You ain't shit. Get the fuck out of my house. I don't know why I thought you would be different. I saw you first, you were supposed to be with me, not her. But since you want to take up for her and be with that ape looking baby, then you can get the fuck out of my house just like Michael," she scolded. Porscha charged at Devon and began hitting him wherever she could make contact with his body. He did all he could to protect himself, but she was swinging so fast, he couldn't block most of her licks.

"Stop hitting me," he instructed her. But Porscha wouldn't listen. She kept swinging on him like he was just some random nigga out there on the streets. Devon grew tired of her hitting him and before he knew it...

**Smack...**

Devon had drawn back and smacked the shit out of Porscha. She was shocked that he'd hit her. She grabbed ahold of her face that was stinging.

"I can't believe you hit me!" she wailed. Devon shrugged his shoulders.

"I told you to stop hitting me," was the only response he could give her.

It was as if the world had come to a complete stop. Nothing moved around them, and no sounds could be heard. Porscha took her hand down from her face and glanced up at the mirror.

Her face had very quickly started to turn red from where she'd been hit. Porscha didn't like that at all. She charged at Devon once more, swinging her arms like she was a windmill.

"Calm your lil' mufuckin' ass down," Devon demanded. He wrapped his arms around Porscha and pulled her as close to him as he could. The tears freely flowed from her eyes. Devon could tell she was still trying to play hard against him, but she was no match for his strength. He glared down into her eyes. She melted into his arms. She sniffled and allowed big alligator sized tears to fall from her eyes, trying her best to still be upset with him. "I do love you," he whispered before placing kisses on her forehead and around her face. He used his hands to smooth back her hair that was sticking up wildly on her head.

Devon placed his lips on top of hers and kissed her with so much passion while his hands roamed up and down her back. She tried to pull away from him, but he wouldn't let her. Instead, he put his hand on top of her head and guided her down to her knees. She glanced up at him with eyes of innocence, but he knew that her innocence had long been lost. He stared into her eyes and undid his pants at the same time. With his dick out, he continued looking at her until she willingly opened her mouth. She wasted no time covering his long, thick dick with her mouth. The minute she sucked on the head of his dick, he allowed a loud moan to escape his mouth.

"Damn, Porscha. I almost forgot what that mouth do," he groaned. He could tell that Porscha was giving him her all with trying to please him

She sucked the head of his dick, flicked her tongue back and forth over it, and then used her hands to play with his balls. That shit always drove him wild. That was something that Porscha did for him that Keyanna didn't do. Porscha always went above and beyond to make sure she left him satisfied.

"Let me get in that pussy. Bend that ass over the bed," he demanded. He didn't have to say it twice. Within a matter of seconds, Porscha had come out of all of her clothes and was on all fours on the edge of the bed. "Naw, fuck that. Let me taste that kitty," he told her. Devon flipped Porscha over and dove head first inside of her pussy. In his mind, she'd better had enjoyed the shit because it was very rare that he'd eat anybody's pussy that wasn't Keyanna.

"Aagggghhhh shitttt..." Porscha hissed as soon as his tongue hit her clit. Her body started bucking, and she was trying to run away from him. He grabbed ahold of her legs and yanked her back toward him. The way he was sucking on her pussy caused her eyes to roll to the back of her head.

"Sssss...." she continued to hiss. When she started to get louder, he knew she was on the verge of cumin' and he wasn't ready for that. He didn't want her to release her nut until he was about to do the same. He flipped her back over and pushed himself inside of her full force. Porscha damn near jumped off the bed trying to get away from him. He tightened his grip and held on to her like he was holding on for dear life.

Devon plunged as deep inside of Porscha as he could go. Porscha started hollering like he was killing her.

"You're too deep," she whined.

"Shut up and take this dick," he instructed her. Porscha closed her mouth and tried to take everything that he was giving her, but when he started pushing deeper inside of her, she threw her hand back, trying to push him back some. It started to irritate Devon. "Come ride this big mufucka then," he directed. Porscha complied with his request.

Devon sat on the edge of the bed while Porscha straddled him. She tried to take her time sliding down his pole, but he got restless and pulled her down the rest of the way.

"Fuckkkk..." she yelled out. He ignored her crying and began pounding up on her from underneath her.

"That's right; ride this muthafucka." He continued to give her orders. Porscha did everything as he requested. He began biting on his bottom lip. He could feel his nut coming up to the tip of his dick. "You 'bout to make a nigga, cum," he commented. He looked up in the shattered mirror and could see a smile appear on Porscha's face. He knew she thought that he was going to cum inside of her, but he was about to show her otherwise. He wasn't about to have a baby with her and wasn't about to risk putting himself in any other situations where they had a close call. As soon as his nut started to spill out, he pushed her off him and caught it in his hand.

"What the fuck?" He heard her say, but he didn't pay her any attention. Devon stood up from the bed and looked back at Porscha.

"Handle your hygiene while I go clean myself up. I gotta find my wife," he told her.

"I know damn well you not about to go looking for that bitch after the moment we just shared," Porscha ranted.

Devon grabbed Porscha around the throat. "Look me in my eyes," he told her. She tried her best to turn away from him, but he only tightened his grip. "You are only some bitch that I'm fuckin'. You will not now nor ever be anything more than that to me. If you disrespect my wife again, I will kill you. Do you understand that?" Devon asked. Porscha nodded her head. "Naw, open your mouth and answer me. I don't read sign language and gestures," he told her.

"Yes!" she hollered.

"Good. Now go clean yourself up; you smell fishy," he quipped. Devon wiped the cum that was in his hand across Porscha's face before he dropped her on the floor. Then he walked over her like she was a piece of trash. He didn't give a damn how he made her feel. All he knew was that he needed to find Keyanna and his son because he didn't trust the streets of Memphis.

### *Chapter Fifteen:*

Michael went down to Beale Street to have a drink. He went to Coyote Ugly because he needed to clear his mind of some of the thoughts that he was having. He was going to return home later that night, but he was going to need a couple of drinks in his system in order to be able to do so.

The way that Porscha acted with him for trying to defend what he'd worked so hard to build was too much for him to handle. He almost felt like she was more worried about protecting Devon than she was about their marriage. It was no secret that there was bad blood between the two men so for Michael to even go out of his way to invite them to come to the house for Porscha's sake should've meant something to her. Now, it seemed that no matter what he did, there was no real way for him to make her happy, and he felt some type of way about that.

"One more round," Michael ordered.

"This is going to be your last one. I can't let you walk out of her drunk like that," the bartender told him.

"Oh, stop acting like you give a damn," Michael slurred.

"Just because I don't know you personally doesn't mean that I don't give a damn," the woman told him and gave him one last shot of tequila.

Michael got up and started dancing on top of the bar. That wasn't out of the ordinary for that bar because people did it all the time. He looked around for a woman that he could take a body shot off of, but all the women seemed like they were taken.

"You trying to do a body shot?" a man walked up to him and asked.

"Not off your mufuckin' ass," Michael replied and laughed.

The man didn't laugh. That showed that he didn't see anything funny. Michael turned away from him and started hollering out all kinds of shit from the bar. The bartender asked him to get down, but he wouldn't do it, so she ended up calling security.

"I'm going, I'm going!" Michael yelled, but he was so drunk, his body didn't budge.

The woman helped him down off the bar and security walked him to the back. A man that Michael thought he'd seen before came over and grabbed him by the arm. Michael tried to snatch away from him, but the man was holding him too tight for him to get loose.

"I got him," the man told security.

"Aye, let me go. I don't know you," Michael hollered, trying to snatch away from the man again.

"I don't give a damn if you know me or not. I know you, and we are about to have a little talk," the man told him. He pulled Michael inside the bathroom and locked the door behind him.

"What the hell are you doing?" Michael asked.

"Shut up and listen," the man told him. Michael watched as the man slammed the toilet seat down and assisted Michael with having a seat. "Now, you don't know me, but I know you. I'm Federal Agent Caldwell, I work for the FBI. We've been watching you for some time now, and I really have all the information I need to throw your black ass under the jail," Agent Caldwell stated. Michael appeared to have sobered up just that quick.

"What the hell did you just say?" Michael questioned him. He wanted to make sure he wasn't just hallucinating.

"I'm sure you heard exactly what I said to you. My men have been watching you for some time, and I know what you've been doing with the money that these dope boys have been giving you. I have more than enough information to lock you away for life, but you're not the one I want."

"Well, who the hell is it that you want?" Michael probed. The agent went into his pocket and pulled out a cell phone. He spent some time scrolling through the phone before he found what he was looking for. He put the phone up in Michael's face so that he could see the picture. "Who the hell is that?" Michael asked, playing dumb.

"You can make this easy on yourself, or you can make it hard. I know you know exactly who this is. Matter fact..." Agent Caldwell paused and showed Michael a picture that he'd taken of Michael speaking with Deuce. Michael suddenly felt sick to his stomach. How the fuck was he going to explain the picture that was before him?

"I don't know him. He just showed up at my office one day," Michael tried to explain.

"That much we know, but he showed up for a reason. You can keep denying all you want to, but we know the truth. I told you that you can either make things harder on yourself or you can make them easy. That's your choice. Now, I'm going to give you some time to sober up. Just remember that we are watching you and will make contact with you again," Agent Caldwell informed him and exited the bathroom. Michael stayed on the toilet trying to figure out what the hell had just happened. He knew he was drunk, but he wasn't that damn drunk to where he didn't understand what was going on. He wanted to reach out to J-Dubb, but he knew that would probably make things worse for him, and he couldn't afford for that to happen.

Michael sat on the toilet a little longer to try to clear his mind. He wasn't in any position to drive, so he pulled out his phone and opened his Uber app. When he'd found one, he walked outside and waited for it to arrive. He'd just come back and get his car the next day. That was if it hadn't been towed by the time he got back. He had to get home because he was not liking the turn of events that had happened in his life in just that one day.

The Uber didn't take long at all to arrive. The driver confirmed the address Michael was going too, which was his home before they pulled away from Beale Street. Michael checked his bank account to see exactly how much money he had in case he needed to go on the run. When he saw that his account was in the negative by a couple of thousand dollars, he felt sick all over again. He then checked the account that he had with Porscha. He was supposed to have a couple million dollars in that account, but there was only a little over two hundred thousand. He hadn't paid their car notes or some of their credit card bills in a few months. There was only going to be a matter of time before Porscha found out about what was going on. He had to do something to stop it.

Had he known that when he started gambling, he would've lost so much of their money, then he wouldn't have ever started. The only reason he kept washing the money for the top dope boys in Memphis was because that was the only way for him to stay afloat. He had Porscha and all of their family thinking that he was this big real estate guru, but he couldn't remember the last time that his ass really sold a house. Everything that he once tried to hide was starting to slowly but surely come to the light. He couldn't imagine the way Porscha would feel once she learned that he'd deceived her all those years. She'd leave him for sure.

"We here, man," the Uber driver alerted Michael. He was so deep in his thoughts that he didn't realize they'd pulled up in front of his house.

"Thanks."

"No problem and feel free to leave me a review and tip," the man suggested.

"I got you," Michael told him and slid out of the car. The only tip he was going to give the man was to not drink and drive. He didn't have shit extra to spare for anybody.

He took his time walking up the steps to his house. He prayed to himself that Porscha was no longer mad at him and would let him back inside the house.

"Porscha?" he called out to her as soon as he entered the home. It looked like everything was still out of place from the fight he'd had with Devon earlier. If he didn't do anything at all the next day, he knew that it would be best for him to go ahead and replace everything he'd fucked up in the house.

"You good?" Devon came from around the corner and asked him.

"Don't act like you care," Michael snapped.

"I really don't. But your wife and my wife are best friends. Even if we don't like each other, the shit that happened today can't happen again. Now, Keyanna done ran out of here pissed at me because of the shit, and I'm worried sick about where she is with my baby."

"She'll be back; they always come back," Michael grunted and headed toward his bedroom. He wasn't in the mood to continue to stand there and make small talk with Devon. He hated Devon with a passion, and he was not going to act no differently toward him.

Inside the room, Porscha was under the covers snoring loudly. Michael wanted to wake her up and talk to her about what happened, but he didn't. It was best for everybody to just let her sleep and that was exactly what he did.

Michael exited the room and slowly closed the door behind him. He went to the kitchen to make a pot of coffee. It would be best for him to sober up a little more before he went to bed or he was going to wake up with an excruciating headache. By the time he had the coffee pot on, Devon popped inside the kitchen with him. Michael carried on about his business as if the nigga weren't standing there.

"Oh, so you gonna get mad at me for ignoring you earlier, but you turn around and do the same shit to me. You know that's childish as fuck, right?"

"Don't talk to me about childish. You came to my crib and disrespected me like I wasn't shit. I know you want what I have, but that ain't gonna happen, nigga."

"There you go with that shit again. Why can't you just accept the fact that we are two niggas that grind for what we want? We both have all that we want and need and are happy with that," Devon pointed out. Michael noticed Devon poke his chest out a little bit. He couldn't do anything but laugh because the shit was stupid as hell. They really didn't know why they couldn't stand each other.

"You right," Michael admitted. "We've been beefing over nothing when we should've been coming together for the sake of our wives," Michael continued.

When Michael's coffee was done, he fixed it how he liked it and took a seat at the table. Devon got up and grabbed him a bottle of water before he took a seat to join Michael at the table. The two men came to the realization that they were both wrong in the situation and were going to have to find a way to get along.

### Chapter Sixteen:

By the time Keyanna made it back to the house, she was exhausted. Exhausted from thinking about everything that happened and fighting with a fussy baby. If she didn't have DJ with her, she would've checked into a hotel and stayed gone for a few days, leaving people to worry about her. That was the old, nonchalant her. The new mother in her guided her conscious and led her to believe that making people worry about her wouldn't be right. Plus, she didn't bring enough milk to get through the night, and she wasn't about to go buy or pump anymore.

Arriving back to the house, DJ was sound asleep. She moved him around as gently as she could because it had taken her forever to get him to fall asleep, and she didn't feel like fussing with him, trying to get him to go back. She was surprised to find the door open when she got to the house. She checked to see if anyone was in the living room before she went on inside. When she didn't see anybody, she took the baby on into the guest room. She changed his diaper and laid him in the basinet before leaving the room and closing the door behind her. She could hear talking in the kitchen so that was the direction she headed in.

Inside the kitchen, the smell of funk and coffee smacked her in the face as soon as she entered. Devon and Michael sat around the table laughing and drinking on whatever. She couldn't believe her eyes. She pinched herself to make sure she wasn't being delusional.

"What the fuck is going on in here?" she finally asked.

"Baby, where the hell have you been? I searched everywhere for you," Devon lied. He stood up and went toward her, but Keyanna jumped back. She didn't want him or anyone else touching on her.

"I guess everywhere stopped at the fuckin' kitchen with yo' lying ass," she refuted. Devon shook his head before turning his water up again. "So y'all supposed to be the best of friends now?"

"Naw, but we knew that we couldn't keep fighting the way that we were. The shit was upsetting Porscha," Devon replied. Michael's brows shot up, but he didn't say anything. He was probably just as curious as Keyanna was about why Devon was so worried about Porscha and not Keyanna.

"Excuse me, but did you say it was upsetting Porscha? What about what the fuck the shit was doing to me? Are you telling me that only her feelings matter?" Keyanna screamed.

"Calm down with all that fuck shit. I said Porscha because we are in her house. Ain't nobody trying to go to jail or be put the fuck out," Devon called himself explaining. Keyanna wasn't buying shit that he was saying.

"You the one on that fuck shit! I can't believe I've stayed married to your selfish ass this long. You're right; we didn't need to have a baby. At least that way, we wouldn't have to worry about custody when we get this fuckin' divorce!" she yelled.

"Keyanna, stop yelling. I'm sure he didn't mean it like that," Michael called himself reasoning with her. "Porscha was the person that I called y'all to come check on because I told y'all she was going through some things. If I asked y'all to come check on her, why would I want y'all up here upsetting her? Damn!" Michael explained. Keyanna still wasn't trying to hear that shit.

"Since y'all are the best of friends, make sure you have somewhere for that nigga to stay when I put him out of my shit." She was still upset about the way that the men had acted, and she was not about to hide her feelings. As far as she was concerned, Devon could've gone out and played in traffic, and she wouldn't have given two fucks. In fact, she ran out of fucks to give last night when he practically told her that he may have cheated on her. That shit waivered in her mind over and over again, and she made a vow to herself that she was going to do her own little investigating to find out the truth, even if it killed her. But, for now, she was going to do her best to play the nice little wife that he expected her to be, so he wouldn't suspect anything.

"You're making a big deal out of nothing. If we can sit here like two civilized individuals and enjoy each other's company, then you shouldn't be worried about what happened earlier. We fucked up, and we know we did. We've talked about it, and we've decided to try our best to get along with each other. At least for as long as you are here. Remember, this shit is for Porscha. I don't know what's going on with her, but if anybody can find out the truth, I know that you can, Keyanna," Michael asserted. Keyanna gave Michael the side-eye because she felt like his ass was just trying to butter her up. Something was up with the two men, and she was going to find out exactly what the hell it was.

"The sad part about all of this is that both of y'all are stupid as fuck," she expressed.

"Hold the fuck up now; there is no need for name calling," Devon stuttered with his words. Him and Michael laughed like he'd just said the funniest shit, but Keyanna just scratched the top of her head.

"No, you hold on. You have your own construction company and this jack ass is supposed to be a top of the line real estate agent. If you had any sense, you'd be working together. When people needed a house built, this idiot could send them to you. But, you're too busy hating each other to think about how you can make money together."

"I told you about all that damn name calling," Devon grunted.

"Oh, you did?" Keyanna marched right over behind him.

**Smack...**

"What the fuck you do that for?" He jumped when he felt her hand go across the back of his neck.

"Because your ass is going to respect me one way or another," she told him. Michael damn near fell out of his chair laughing at the two of them bickering back and forth with each other.

"That's how me and Porscha used to be. At one point, we were the life of the party. Now, all she does is walk around here worried about her makeup business and if we got money," Michael sadly admitted. Keyanna stared at him because she could hear the sadness all in his voice. She was shocked that he'd even said as much as he did because he was never the type of person that would admit his feelings. Both he and Porcha had faked the funk so long of having everything together, that neither of them realized how plastic they really acted.

"Don't talk about me like I'm not here." Everyone froze at the sound of Porscha's voice. "Why you getting quiet now? You had a lot to say when you thought I was sleep," she chirped.

"It's not even like that," Michael confessed.

"Then what is it like? Go ahead and tell me and everyone else what your problem is with me."

"I don't have a problem with you. I have a problem with the way our relationship has changed. Everything seems to solely be about money for you."

"That's because we need money to survive. You had money before you met me, so why not have it while we are together?" Porscha questioned.

"That's the problem. I had money before you, and evidently, I wasn't happy just having that money, which is why I quickly put a ring on it when I met you. If I was happy just with having that money, then trust me when I tell you that I would've been out there still living the single life. If you aren't going to be the wife that I married you for, then there is no need for us to still be together. You know... the one that loves me unconditionally, stands behind me in public even when I'm wrong, corrects my ass in private, and supports the hell out of me, then I don't want that," Michael truthfully spoke. Keyanna looked between the both of them and wondered if that was the alcohol talking or if Michael truly felt that way.

Porscha opened her mouth to say something, but Michael pushed right past her and headed for their room. Porscha looked defeated, but she didn't say anything. Keyanna knew that she'd be able to get her to talk about it tomorrow, when it was just the two of them.

"Goodnight y'all," Porscha finally spoke and left out of the kitchen behind Michael.

"We need to be getting some sleep too," Devon advised, pushing up on Keyanna.

"Don't be pushing up on me like you're about to get some. Sleep is all you are going to be getting tonight," she assured him.

"Damn, I know you not still trippin' about earlier. I've done all that I can to apologize."

"There's one more thing I need you to do," she told him. "Come on to the room," she directed. He smiled.

"About time you 'bout to let a nigga get off in that."

"Naw, I'm not about to let you get off in shit. But, you 'bout to let a bitch smell your dick," she advised. He stood there for a brief moment. She took it that it hadn't registered to him what she'd just requested.

See, when Porscha pushed passed them to follow Michael, she smelled a certain scent that she hadn't smelled before. Then, when Devon walked up on her, she smelt that same scent again. She was a lot of things, but a damn fool wasn't one of them. All hell was going to break lose if she learned that what she was thinking to be true, really happened.

### Chapter Seventeen:

The next morning, Porcha woke up with a pounding headache. She felt around in the bed and realized that Michael wasn't there. She got up and went into the bathroom. Opening the medicine cabinet, she took down a bottle of Tylenol. After running water in one of the glasses she kept in the bathroom, she tossed two pills in her mouth and chased it down with the water.

**Tap... Tap...**

"Who is it?" she called out when she heard someone tapping on her bedroom door.

"It's me, sis," Keyanna replied, sticking her head in the door so that Porscha would know for sure that it was her.

"What's up, sis?"

"Let's get out of here. I'm going to leave the baby with Devon, so we can have a little time to ourselves," Keyanna asserted.

"That's fine with me. Let me get dressed, and I'll be ready to go. Plus, I haven't been shopping in a while. That would be nice to do while we play catch-up."

Keyanna left out the room to get dressed. Porscha jumped in the shower since she didn't really have time to do it the night before after her session with Devon. As soon as she was about to, she heard Michael come trampling in the house, so she had to throw the covers over her head and pretend to be sleep. She didn't want him to try to have sex with her right after another man had been inside of her not even ten minutes earlier.

Michael got up early this morning with an attitude. It was no doubt in her mind that his attitude was because of what she'd revealed last night. She hated that he thought she was with him for money, but truth was, she wasn't happy anymore. She truly was in love with Devon, but she knew that he wasn't going to leave Keyanna for her. Even if he did, they'd never be able to be happy together because Keyanna could be grimy and would stop at nothing to make their lives a living hell when someone hurt her.

Porscha did a spot clean where she cleaned under her arms and between her legs before exiting the shower. She took some time to clean up the mess she'd made in their room before throwing on a long maxi dress and some Old Navy flip flops. She normally dressed better than that, but she wasn't in the mood to be cute. That and she figured that Keyanna didn't have as much money as them, so she wouldn't be dressed in name brand clothes from head to toe. More than likely, she'd be in something she got from Citi Trends or Rainbow.

"I'm ready," Keyanna sang as she came prancing to the door again.

"Come on in," Porscha instructed her. She really wanted to see what the hell Keyanna was wearing. Porscha's eyes got big as hell when she saw Keyanna rocking a Gucci dress that looked like a long-collared shirt and some Gucci flip flops. Her hair was thrown up in a messy ponytail and she had on light makeup.

"Why you looking at me like that? You want me to change?"

"Naw, you good. I'm the one that needs to change," Porscha suggested.

"Don't nobody care about your Citi Trends dress. Let's go," Keyanna commented. *Did this bitch just throw a whole fuckin' palm tree at me?* Porscha asked herself. Keyanna was good about throwing shade, but at other people. Porscha really didn't know how to react when she did it to her, but she kept her mouth shut to keep herself from saying the wrong thing.

*Next time, I'ma let her know how her husband was busting this pussy open*, Porscha thought to herself, smiling at her friend. She felt some type of way about Keyanna's comment, but she wasn't going to act on it until the time was right.

Keyanna and Porscha got inside of Porscha's Mercedes and headed to the outlets that were in Southaven.

"You come way out here to go shopping?" Keyanna asked Porscha.

"You know the outlets be having different shit and their prices are better."

"Since when have you ever cared about the price of something?" Keyanna questioned. Porscha took that as another shot.

"Keep on, bitch," she muttered.

"What you say?"

"Nothing. I was just thinking out loud," Porscha replied.

The two women dipped in and out of the different stores. Keyanna seemingly was picking up more stuff than Porscha was. It wasn't until they got inside of the Michael Kors store that Porscha really start picking things up. She got several purses with the matching wallets and a pair of shoes. After handing the merchandise to the cashier, she handed her a credit card and continued to look around the store in case there was something else she wanted.

"Excuse me, ma'am," the cashier came toward Porscha roughly five minutes later. "I'm sorry to tell you, but this card was declined." The woman called herself trying to whisper, but Porscha was too ashamed about the card declining to notice. She thought the woman was trying to make her look bad in front of the other customers in the store. Truth was, she wasn't even worried about looking bad in front of the other bitches; it was Keyanna that she didn't want to see her in a bad way.

"This some muthafuckin' bullshit, run it again," she yelled at the cashier.

"Ma'am, I've ran the card three times, and it has declined all three times." She noticed that the cashier had started raising her voice as well.

"Keep it together, sis. You're making a scene," Keyanna told her, but Porscha didn't give a damn. They had plenty of money, so it had to be the store's system that was making her look like a fuckin' fool.

"I'm going to sue the fuck out of you and this store for embarrassing me."

"You're embarrassing yourself by getting loud with me. Now, you can take that bass out your voice and talk to me like you got some sense or we can keep going back and forth with each other and making it obvious to the other customers in this store that your ass is broke," the cashier hissed.

Porscha was about to respond when she saw one of the members of her church coming toward her. She snatched the card from the woman, grabbed Keyanna by the arm and tried to move away from the register before the woman reached her. She apparently didn't move fast enough because when she turned around, she ran smack into the woman.

"Is everything alright over here, Porscha?" the woman questioned her.

"Yes, Mrs. Mims; everything is fine. There is something wrong with their credit card machine," Porscha assured the woman.

"Well, that's funny because I just used my card at two different registers and I didn't have any problems. Did you give them the right card?" Mrs. Mims snidely commented.

"Look you ole uppity bitch, you need to mind yo' mufuckin' business." Before Porscha knew it, she'd snapped on the woman. Mrs. Mims grabbed ahold of her chest like she was clutching on some pearls. "Now, if you know what's good for you, you better get your Michelin Man built ass out of my face," Porscha spat.

"I'll pay for it," Keyanna stated and handed the woman her credit card. Porscha realized she was only trying to save face, but she wasn't with taking charity from no damn body. The cashier handed Keyanna the bags and she passed them over to Porscha.

"Thank you," Porscha said just above a whisper. She was so outdone with the whole situation that she couldn't even look Keyanna in the face.

"Come on, sis. I want to go into one other store," Keyanna told Porscha. However, Porscha had different plans.

"No, we are going to Michael's job to get this shit straightened out right the fuck now," Porscha commented. Keyanna didn't argue with her. That was only because everyone knew when Porscha had her mind made up about something, there was no changing it.

Porscha moved so fast getting out of the store that she damn near knocked about ten people down. She got into it with two other people, and she almost got slapped by another.

"These bitches just don't know who they fuckin' with," Porscha ranted.

By the time they made it to the car, someone had called the police. Porscha had a feeling they were looking for her, so she opted to stay in her parking spot. She wasn't going to move until the police were no longer in sight. She noticed that Keyanna sat there with no words, yet she was shaking her head at her. She was going to ask her what that was about, but she didn't feel like getting into it with anyone else.

### *Chapter Eighteen:*

When Michael arrived at his office this morning, he had an unexpected visitor. Deuce was sitting in the waiting area like it was natural for him to be there. Michael held his briefcase up to his face and tried to walk right past Deuce, but that didn't work. In fact, Deuce threatened to kick Michael's ass all throughout the office if he didn't show him a little more respect.

Michael stormed into his office despite the fact that Angelique was talking to him. *Whatever she has to say to me can wait*, he thought to himself.

"You just don't understand how serious this situation is," Deuce barked. He slammed Michael's door shut once he was inside the office with him.

"No, you don't understand how serious this shit is. I went out to get a drink last night and was approached by a fuckin' federal agent. I'm not trying to go to jail for no gotdamn body," Michael growled.

"Nigga, who the fuck is you talking to like that?" Before Michael knew it, Deuce had yoked his ass up. He was in the air with his feet dangling beneath him. He tried to say something, but the way Deuce was holding him, he couldn't get anything out. Hell, he had to fight to even try to breath.

Deuce pushed Michael over to the window and began opening it up. Michael squirmed like a fish out of water. His eyes damn near bulged out of his head when he saw what was about to happen.

Deuce held Michael out of the window by his feet. His body moved around like he was a piece of meat being dangled in front of its prey.

"Come on, man. I'm trying to tell you that we are being watched."

"Fuck that shit. You trying to tell me that you don't want to work with me after I've already told you that ain't an option."

"I heard you, but I can't. The Feds are going to take both of us down. I'm trying to help you."

"Who the fuck are you, Tina Turner? You trying to help Ike now?" Deuce grunted. Michael didn't know what to say or do. The only thing he could do was yell and plead with Deuce to not drop him.

**Bam... Bam... Bam...**

"Is everything alright in there?" Angelique beat on the door, distracting Deuce. Michael was no fool. He was fully aware of the fact that Deuce could kill him in front of a room full of people and neither of them would open their mouth to tell a soul because they'd be too scared to.

"Help me..." he cried out.

Angelique pushed the door open. Her hands flew to her mouth when she saw what was going on.

"May I help you?" Deuce asked her as if he weren't doing anything wrong.

"Naw, this ain't got shit to do with me. Matter fact, I'm going home for the rest of the day," she told him. Angelique left back out of the office and closed the door.

"You see how quick she was to leave you in here with me? You should see now that I have a lot of fuckin' pull and that's just your damn secretary. You can tell me no again and see won't I drop your ass," Deuce informed Michael.

"I'm sorry. I won't ever tell you no again," Michael spoke. He begged Deuce to let him go. He could feel himself getting dizzy as blood rushed to the top of his head.

"Wake yo' bitch ass up," Deuce ordered. He pulled Michael inside the window and slapped him around a few times. "Fuck you sleeping for?" Deuce questioned. Apparently, he hadn't realized that the blood rushin' to Michael's head fucked him up.

"Damn, Boss Man; this nigga done pissed on himself." The same man that was with Deuce the last time was with him again. He was killing himself laughing at the way Michael suddenly became a bitch at the hands of Deuce.

"Sho' in the fuck did. How the hell you a grown ass man and can't even hold your piss?" Deuce chuckled.

"I have a bad bladder," Michael lied. "You need to get out of here," he directed Deuce who wouldn't budge. The only thing Deuce did after standing there and looking at him for a few moments was have a seat in front of Michael's desk. "I told you to leave. Do it now before I call security," he warned Deuce.

"You think you scare me? Nigga, ain't no bitch in my blood. I am mufuckin' security."

Michael marched over to the door. He held it open with the hopes of Deuce getting up and leaving without causing any more problems. The only thing he got when he opened the door was an angry Porscha. He heard Angelique yelling and trying to stop her, but Porscha kept walking.

"Can you do your fuckin' job?" Michael stuck his head out the door and yelled at Angelique.

"Don't be taking your anger out on me. Seems that you've pissed two people off, and I'd hate to be you right about now!" Angelique screamed. Michael stood in the doorway and watched as she gathered her purse and went to the elevator. "I don't need this shit," she told him. "I quit!" She stepped on the elevator without looking back.

Michael grabbed ahold of his head. He had a sudden headache and didn't know how to get rid of it. With the look on Porscha's face, he got a feeling that the headache would not be going away any time soon.

"What do you want, Porscha?"

"I want you to tell me why the fuck I go to the outlet to do a little shopping with Keyanna and my damn card declined."

"Did you tell her to run the card again?"

"Do I look fuckin' stupid to you? Of course, I told her to run it again, and she said she ran it three times."

"Maybe they put a block on the card when they kept running it. You know how the bank is," he tried to explain.

"Nigga, don't try me. What the fuck is wrong with the accounts? And the bank ain't got shit to do with this. This was my fuckin' credit card. Did you pay the bill?" she questioned him.

"Which credit card did you try?"

"The fuckin' credit card that I always use."

"Is it the same exact one that you've been using to fund your little makeup business? The same one that you use to pay bills with? The same one your ass spends from and never think to put money back on it?" Michael asked her a set of his own questions.

"Don't be questioning me in front of all these damn people." Michael looked around to see exactly who "all" those people were she was referring to. Wasn't nobody in the office but him, her, Deuce, and that big ass nigga Deuce had come in with him.

"You came in here questioning me. Don't do shit to me that you don't want done to you. Now, you need to get your shit together and leave. I have important business matters to tend to. I'll put money on the card when I get home," he told her.

"No, you will put money on the fuckin' card now and you will give me extra money so that I can go do some more shopping to make up for the fact that you embarrassed me."

"Did I embarrass you or did you embarrass yourself by swiping a card without checking to see if it actually had money on it?"

"Fuck you, Michael!" she hollered. "And who the fuck are you?" Michael saw the way Porscha glanced over at Deuce, and he didn't like it one bit. He almost thought he saw her licking her lips, but since he didn't actually see that, he didn't say anything.

"Where is Keyanna?"

"She's in the car waiting on me."

"Go home, Porscha. I will deal with this bullshit later. I have work to do." Michael was really trying to get Porscha out of the office so he could find a way to deal with Deuce.

"Fine. But you better bring your ass straight to the house when you're done," she chided.

"Here lil' momma. This is some money I was about to give your husband for a deal, but it looks to me as if I need to be letting you handle the money." Deuce laughed and stretched his arm out to hand the money to Porscha. Michael snatched the money out of Deuce's hand. That was the wrong move because it made Deuce jump up like he was about to fight. Michael threw his hand up like he was surrendering before anything went down.

"Damn, you really are a punk bitch. I got more balls than you," Porscha remarked.

"Porscha, go home now. And don't bring your ass back to my office being all dramatic and causing a scene," Michael instructed her, pointing toward the door.

"Fine. Asshole!" Porscha grunted and pushed past Michael. He kept his eyes on her the entire time. He felt a sense of relief when he saw her step on the elevator and the doors closed behind her.

"You can leave as well," he commented to Deuce.

"Oh, I know I can, and I'm about to. It's a shame that this may have been the last time you were able to look at your wife's beautiful face."

"What? You better not go near my wife!"

"I've been near her once, and I'm sure that won't be the last time. You can keep telling me that you aren't going to work with me and see how quickly your wife disappears." Deuce winked at Michael before laughing. He left out the door once he'd given Michael his last and final warning. That was when Michael accepted the fact that he had no choice but to either help Deuce or Agent Caldwell.

Michael pulled the card out of his wallet that he'd gotten from the federal agent the night before. What he was about to do was going to be life changing and could get him killed, but he had to do something. Being around Deuce was not only a danger to him, but the other people in his life. He couldn't let that shit go down like that.

"I'm in," was the only thing Michael said to the federal agent after he heard him pick the phone up.

Michael hung up without giving him a chance to respond and then stood from his desk. He was headed home to Porscha. What he had agreed to do may have cost him his wife, but he'd rather her be safe than dead.

### *Chapter Nineteen:*

Porscha got back to the house and was still angry about what happened at the outlet. There was no way she could let the shit go because she was too embarrassed.

"Go get you a nap in. I need to check into a few things. I also have a Skype meeting with a potential client in about thirty minutes," she informed Keyanna.

"Aight, sis. I'll see you in a bit. I need to go check on my two men anyway," Keyanna responded. She cheerfully waltzed out of the room to go check on DJ and Devon.

Porscha made sure nobody was watching her and stepped inside of the room that Michael had been using as an office. She pulled out her phone and took a picture of the way everything was in the office, so she'd know how to put the shit back before she went straight over to his desk and started pulling out all of the papers that he had in there. She rummaged through them to see if she could find anything that would let her know exactly how much money they had. By the way the card declined in the mall and the way Michael acted when she was at his office, she knew that something was going on that she was not aware of. Whatever it was, she told herself that she was going to get to the bottom of it and confront him for lying before she left him.

Yeah, Porscha had one degree, was in school for a second degree, and was working on her own business. However, when she met Michael, he had money and vowed to take care of her for the rest of her life. That was one of the main reasons she gave him a chance. Now she was seeing that it was all a dream and all of the nightmares she was having were really warnings to the fact that they may have been broke.

After going through all of the paperwork in his desk and not finding anything, she went over to his file cabinet. Of course, he was smart enough to keep the drawers locked, but she knew there was a key around there somewhere. She looked inside of every trinket that he had on his shelves and even started throwing books off his bookshelf before a key fell out.

"Bingo," she yelled. She hurried to cover her mouth and hoped that no one heard her. She wouldn't be able to explain to Keyanna or Devon why she was going through shit in her husband's office, so she knew she needed to be as discreet as she possibly could.

Porscha put the book that the key fell out of on top of the file cabinet, so she'd remember to put it back inside of it. She was happy once she put the key inside of the file cabinet and it unlocked. She started pulling all of the papers out. When she came to a file that was labeled "bank", she smiled because she was going to find out exactly how much money they had; or so she thought. Porscha read over every sheet of paper that was in the folder. She was in disbelief when she saw that they were really broke. One of their bank accounts was in the negative and another one had a notice for closure because it hadn't had any money in it for a few months. They were behind on their car payments, the credit card bills, and the mortgage. She even saw a notice indicating that their house was up for foreclosure. She suddenly felt sick to her stomach.

"What the fuck is going on?" she asked herself. Tears built up in her eyes and had threatened to fall but she did whatever she could to prevent that from happening. She couldn't cry over lies that she'd been told. She had to find a way to get even.

***Knock... Knock...***

"Damn, is there not a such thing as privacy around this bitch anymore?" she hollered.

"I'm sorry, sis. I was just checking to see if you were okay. I kept hearing a loud commotion and then you hollered out something," Keyanna stated, sticking her head inside the office door.

"Yeah, I'm just trying to finalize some paperwork before I have my meeting later. Everything okay with you?" she inquired, trying to play it cool.

"Yeah. DJ is sleeping of course, so Devon and I are about to go out to grab a bite to eat. Is that fine with you?"

"If you're asking me to watch my Godson, you know you don't even have to ask. I'd love to spend a little one-on-one time with him," she offered.

"Thank you so much, sis. You just don't know how much I appreciate you," Keyanna expressed. She ran and gave Porscha a big hug before running back out of the room.

Porscha pulled out her phone and took a picture of everything she'd found. She sent the pictures to her email and an attorney she'd been working with to start her business. She busied herself returning everything back to the file cabinet. She had to keep looking back at the pictures in her phone to make sure she put everything back where it belonged. With any luck, if she put something out of place and Michael were to come in and check on things, he'd think he was in such a rush to put the shit back that he didn't do it in any particular order.

As Porscha was about to leave the office, she decided that she wanted a physical copy of the paperwork. She had pictures, but anybody could say that she used Photoshop to develop those pictures, and she didn't have time for that. When she laid everything on the table, she wanted to have solid proof. She sat her phone down on the desk and turned on the video recorded. Step by step, she went back over to the file cabinet and pulled the folder out that held everything that she needed. She called out everything that she was doing to make sure it was on tape. She had to stop a few times to adjust the camera to show everything. She didn't want anything to be questionable. With the printer/copy/fax machine in the room, she ran two copies of the paperwork and faxed a copy over to her attorney. She was waiting for a confirmation sheet to come through until she heard a door slam.

"Porschaaaaaa..." Michael called out to her. She remained silent because if she would've responded to him, he would've known that she was in his office. While she waited for that confirmation to come through, she dashed through the office putting everything back in the folder the way she remembered them being in there.

*Beep...*

The fax machine beeped while she was getting ready to put the key to the file cabinet back inside of the book that it fell from. She jogged over to it and hit the button to silence it, but it was no use because the paper she'd been waiting for started coming through.

"Shit! Think, Porscha," she said to herself. She began hitting herself in the head with the book that she'd been holding.

"Porschaaaaaa..." Michael called out to her once again. She darted over to the door and listened for his footsteps. They seemed far away which led her to believe that he'd gone to their bedroom to see if she was there. She picked her phone up from the desk and sent Keyanna a text for assistance.

*Porscha: Stall Michael! I'll explain everything later.*

She put her ear to the door and waited for Keyanna's phone to go off. She'd forgotten all about the fact that Keyanna was leaving the house with Devon. The sound of Michael's footsteps getting closer to her told her that Keyanna wasn't available to help her. She was pissed.

Porscha put the book in her hand back on the shelf and checked to make sure the trinkets and everything else appeared to be in order, to the best of her ability. She ran behind the desk and straightened it out, making sure that she put everything back inside of their perspective drawers. Porscha glanced up as Michael entered the office.

"What are you doing in here?" he prodded. He started surveying his office. She already knew he was trying to see if anything was out of place. That's when she saw the shiny key still sitting in the file cabinet from when she unlocked it. Her nerves got the best of her and her heart seemed to have dropped to the floor.

"I needed to fax something off." She was glad that she was smart enough to put all of her copies inside of a folder of its own, so he couldn't see what all she had.

"But why are you in here? You have a fax machine and everything else that you need in your own damn office," he bickered.

"I came in here hoping you would come home early. I wanted to apologize to you for the way that I acted earlier. You had clients in there, and I was wrong. I just wanted you to feel the way I did when my card declined," she somewhat lied. She couldn't care less about the fact that there were clients in his office. She was however, pissed at him for snatching the money away from her that the man was trying to give her. In her mind, it was rightfully hers.

"And you should apologize. You showed your natural black ass for no reason. When I told you that I would handle things when I got home, you should've taken my word for it. We can't be together if you aren't going to trust me," he fussed. She looked him upside his head the entire time he talked. Everything that he said went in one ear and out the other.

"You're right." She smiled and made her way over to him. Porscha wrapped her arms around his neck and kissed all over him. "Go upstairs and get comfortable. I'm going to see if Keyanna and Devon will go to a hotel tonight, so we can have the house all to ourselves."

"No, don't worry about it. I know they don't want to have DJ in a hotel because he's still so young. I wouldn't blame them because of all these germs these hotels have floating around them."

"That's fine. We can go to the hotel. Let me call and get everything set up there for us, and I'll let you know all of the plans a little later. Go pack an overnight bag. Although, I wouldn't pack a lot of clothes because they are going to be off more than they are on," she seductively spoke to him. She rubbed on his head the entire time she was talking to him because she knew how relaxed that made him.

"Word?" He smiled and watched as she nodded her head yes. Michael was about to leave out of the office but paused in his tracks. She thought she was screwed. There was no way he didn't see the key sticking out of the damn file cabinet. "Oh, and please hurry up, and get out of my office. You know how anal I am about you touching my shit."

"You don't be saying that shit when I'm touching your dick and it's stuff."

"But, that's different. It's stuff that we share together."

"Just like everything else in this house," she muttered.

"Something like that. Now, let me go get ready and you bring yo' fine ass on," he asserted.

Michael grabbed Porscha by the waist and moved her right along with him out of the office. It seemed that he was aware that she was up to something or he was really doing his best to keep his secrets in the dark, but she was on to him.

"Let me tell Keyanna what we're about to do and I'll be on in there. Go pack," she instructed him. Michael gave her a kiss on the lips and left her standing by the room Keyanna and Devon were in. She used that time to grab the confirmation sheet off the fax machine and stick it in her folder, she locked the file cabinet back, and put the key back inside the book and stuck it on the shelf. She then ran to the guest room to check on DJ because she figured Devon and Keyanna were already gone to eat.

Porscha didn't knock on the door because she was inside her home. She pushed the door open and found Keyanna on her knees, giving Devon head.

"What the fuck? Wasn't y'all supposed to be gone to get something to eat? I come in here to check on the baby and you in here suckin' dick." Porscha had to catch herself. Devon smirked and took his time pulling his pants up. Keyanna jumped up to her feet and started wiping her mouth.

"Sorry, sis. I wasn't trying to disrespect you in your home. You know how it is when you can't please your man sexually, so you have to think of other ways to make him happy."

"Naw, I don't know shit about that because I'd suck and fuck my man like my life depended on it regardless to what was going on with me."

"Hold the fuck up. You need to calm down, sis," Keyanna barked. She strutted over to Porscha like she was about to punch the shit out of her. Porscha did notice that Keyanna's hands were balled up.

"You seem like you have a problem with me suckin' my husband's dick. Maybe if you'd been doing the same to Michael, his ass would remember to pay those bills on time."

"What you say to me, bitch?"

"You heard exactly what I said. You're my girl, but you not about to keep throwing side shots at me like I'm a problem. I haven't done a damn thing to you. Hell, if I wanna shove my husband's dick down my mouth then I will. I'm so deep throated, I'll stick his dick and balls in my mouth and lick his ass all at the same mufuckin' time." Porscha was fuming, but she couldn't let that show. "Matter fact, get the fuck out. We 'bout to work on baby number two. You'd know how to do that if you weren't so selfish and actually gave a damn about giving Michael a baby." Keyanna shoved Porscha out of the room. She didn't even give her the opportunity to say anything back to her. Porscha was ready to fight, but she had to keep her composure. She was going to handle Keyanna in due time.

"What was all of that noise?" Michael questioned Porscha when she stepped inside of their room.

"That was Keyanna. She on some bitch shit because I walked in and caught her suckin' dick."

"What's wrong with that?"

"She's suckin' dick in our house; I'm the only one in this house that should be suckin' anyone's dick."

"Yeah, you should but you barely do that. Since she not fuckin' right now, let her suck the skin off his dick. You need to be worried about all the shit we're going to be doing to each other when we get to this hotel room," Michael boasted.

Porscha rolled his eyes without him seeing it. When he turned his back, she slid the folder she'd been holding in her hand between their mattress. She hated that she told Michael she was going to fuck him because she suddenly felt disgusted with the thought of him touching her. She started to wonder to herself how she was going to get out of the bullshit she'd gotten herself into.

### Chapter Twenty:

"Stupid bitch!" Keyanna screamed and punched the wall. She wished it was Porscha's face.

"Damn, Key; don't put a hole in these folks wall." Devon laughed.

"Fuck that bitch and her cheap ass wall." Keyanna started mumbling to herself while Devon sat back and laughed. "This shit not funny. I'm sick of her ass always having shit to say about somebody else's relationship. Hell, if she'd get on her knees more for Michael's Hunchback of Notre Dame lookin' ass then she probably wouldn't be having all those damn problems in her marriage," Keyanna snapped.

"What problems do they have in their marriage? Let them tell it, everything is peaches n' cream."

"She's a peaches n' cream mufuckin' lie. I didn't tell you this, but we went shopping earlier and the hoe's card declined. She caused a scene in the damn store. I went ahead and paid for her items because she must've wanted them real bad to act the way that she did."

"How much did you spend? That bitch name ain't Charity and that's the only person I make donations too," Devon fumed.

"Stop trying to be funny. I'm being serious, Devon."

"You can seriously finish suckin' this dick. I'm not about to not get my nut because you and ole girl beefing over some dumb shit. Come suck this dick like a porn star and I might give you an award later."

"Naw, fuck all that. Come lick this pussy like it's cotton candy," she shot back. Devon stared at her like he was debating over whether he really wanted to do it or not.

Devon leaned in and placed a kiss of Keyanna's lips. It was one of pure passion. He moved her body around to the bed as he continued to kiss her. She closed her eyes and enjoyed the pleasure she was receiving from just his touch alone. Devon pushed her down on the bed and her eyes popped open.

"Chill out, ma. I'm not going to hurt you," he told her. She watched as he slithered his way down her body to her thighs. He snatched her dress open and began kissing all over her thighs. She exhaled, feeling her pussy getting wet. It was too soon to her for them to be having sex, but she didn't know how much longer she'd be able to go without feeling him inside of her.

Nervousness ran throughout her body. The moment Devon's tongue touched her pearl, she exhaled again. She was used to pleasuring him, but it had been a while since he returned the gesture. Keyanna spread her legs wider so she could feel as much of his tongue inside of her as possible. Her moans became louder as he pulled back and licked around her pussy. With her eyes closed, she used her hands and guided him right back to her center.

"Oooo... Don't stop, baby," she cried out. Keyanna was experiencing the best feeling in the world as Devon sucked and slurped on her pussy. Keyanna's legs began to tremble beyond her control.

"How that shit feel, baby?" Devon stopped to ask her, but she didn't answer him. She didn't have time for questions because she knew she was about to cum. So, once again, she put her hand on his head and guided his tongue back to her pussy.

Devon sucked on her shit like it was a popsicle. Her eyes rolled to the back of her head as she enjoyed the pleasure she was receiving. Her moans got louder, and she couldn't take it anymore.

"I'm about to cummmmm... Mmmmm... Don't stop, Devon," she requested.

"Naw, we bustin' in this bitch together," he told her. Keyanna's eyes popped open again. She watched as Devon jumped up and removed his pants. He crawled in between her legs and ushered himself inside of her slowly.

"Ohhhhh..." she gasped, trying to hide the pain she was feeling. It had been so long since they had sex that she'd tightened up a little more than she already was. Once he was inside of her, she wiggled her body around some to adjust to his dick's size and width.

"Why you moving like a snake?" he asked, flashing a big ass grin.

"Because this snake just swallowed a big ass mouse, and I'm trying to work him all the way down to the bottom of my stomach," she replied. That was her way of telling him she wanted all that dick inside of her.

"Your wish is my command," he responded. Right then, Devon pushed all of himself inside of her. Keyanna almost yelled out until she turned her head to the side and saw the ugly ass pink wall coloring and remembered that they weren't at their house.

Devon took his time stroking inside of her. Keyanna sensed he was enjoying it as much as she was by the way he was licking his lips and kept closing his eyes. Throughout their sex session, Devon would nibble or suck on her neck and nipples. She loved when he called himself being rough because she liked when he took the lead during sex. He'd passionately kiss her and grab a handful of her hair.

"That dick feels so good, baby. Why you been keeping it from me?" Keyanna inadvertently asked.

"The fuck? I ain't kept shit from you. You the one that's been stingy with the pussy. I almost took that shit a few times." Devon stopped stroking long enough to tell her.

"I'm sorry, baby. You'll never have to worry about that shit again because this dick is too much to be missing out on," she assured him. She started moving her body underneath him to get him back going with his stroking.

Devon slid his arms underneath her and cuffed her under her arms. He placed his body down on top of hers and began grinding on her pussy.

"Why you doing this to me?" she cried out.

"So, you won't have time to think about letting another nigga do it. This my mufuckin' pussy, and it'll always be mine," he asserted. Keyanna nodded her head in agreement. After the shit Devon was doing to her, she couldn't think about another man. "I love you so much, Keyanna," he whispered in her ear. That was all the confirmation to her that he was all she ever needed.

"I love you too," she replied as they both released their juices.

Keyanna didn't care if she'd gotten pregnant or not because she at least knew she was with the man she was going to spend the rest of her life with.

### Chapter Twenty-One:

Devon tiptoed down the hallway to the bathroom while he was still naked. He wanted to take a shower so he could feel refreshed, but he had plans on getting some more pussy later that night. In his mind, they had a lot of catching up to do. Keyanna was in the room tending to DJ while Devon was in the bathroom. His phone rang, so he stuck his head out the door and checked to see if anyone was in the hallway before he answered the call.

"What's up?" he greeted his old college buddy, Reginald.

"Not shit. What you got going on?" Reginald replied.

"Man... I'm so ready to get the fuck away from here, you don't even know."

"You've only been there for a day and a half," Reginald chuckled.

"And that was more than enough time to know that I can't deal with no bullshit ass nigga for too long. I know I said I would help you out, but I can't. I got to get my wife out of this house. Then, the nigga had the nerve to put his pissy ass fat fingers on me. I tried to stomp a hole in his ass."

"Don't damage the merchandise," Reginald told him. "Besides, pretty soon, we will have more than enough to put his ass away."

Devon thought about what Reginald had said to him. It almost made him regret trying to get Michael out of the picture.

Especially, since they decided they could work together and both be getting money; thanks to Keyanna's suggestion.

Reginald and Devon went to school together. They linked up one night that Reginald was in town, and Reginald ended up telling him about a case that he was working on. Devon intently listened to his friend until Reginald slipped up and said Michael's name. Devon asked Reginald to show him a picture of Michael, and when he did, he was able to confirm that it was Porscha's husband. Devon thought about saying something to Reginald that night about knowing Michael, but it wasn't until Porscha called him a few days later venting about some bullshit ass dreams she was having that Devon decided it was time to get rid of Michael. He figured he could get Porscha to move in with him and Keyanna so that he could have both of his women under the same roof. Now, he hated the fact that he went as far as telling Reginald that he had a connection to Michael and could possibly get some information on him that could help send him away. Michael calling and asking them to come visit was just icing on the cake. That was the best way for Devon to get inside of their home without people being suspicious. Keyanna would've known that he was on some bullshit if he would've offered to just bring her to Tennessee.

"Damn, bro; you listening to me?"

"Yeah, my bad. I was just thinking about something. What did you say?"

"I said that you don't need to damage the merchandise," Reginald repeated.

"I didn't. I'm just worried about how this could backfire on me. The nigga married to my wife's best friend, and even though I can't stand his ass, I don't want to tear their family apart," Devon conscientiously spoke.

"Then what was the point of you even reaching out to me and agreeing to help?"

**Knock... Knock...**

"Is everything okay in there, baby?" Keyanna knocked on the door to check on Devon.

"Uh, yeah, baby," he stuttered. "My stomach is a little messed up. We are going to have to get something to eat," he continued.

"Okay, you hurry up in there so I can get cleaned up or we can do it together." Keyanna pushed the door open.

*Damn, I forgot to lock the door*, Devon wanted to hit himself in the head.

"What the fuck are you doing?" Keyanna snapped when she saw Devon propped up on the bathroom counter with the phone glued to his ear.

"I'm about to get in the shower, what does it look like?"

"You've been in this bathroom well over five minutes, and the shower isn't even on. It looks to me like you came in here to take a private call."

"Private call? Why would I need to take a private call?" he hollered. He was trying to make it seem like he was disputing what she was saying when he was really trying to think of a real way to cover his ass.

"Don't play with me, Devon. I swear you're going to make me fuck you up," Keyanna threatened. Devon noticed her slowly moving closer and closer to him. He wanted to step back, but there was nowhere for him to move.

Unexpectedly, Keyanna snatched Devon's phone out of his hand. He was surprised at the way she was acting. His hand was still held up to his ear like his phone was there, and he had a shocked expression on his face. He was in too much disbelief to even say anything to her and silently prayed that Reginald wouldn't say anything that would give away what he was really doing.

"Look, bitch; I don't know who the fuck this is or why you think I won't fuck you up, but you better quit calling my fuckin' husband's phone. Whatever y'all think y'all had going on is over and done with," Keyanna barked in the phone. She put it on speaker so that whenever the person replied, they could hear them together.

"Excuse me. I can assure you that I don't want your husband," Reginald replied.

"It's a man!" Keyanna's hands flew up to her mouth, causing the phone to fall to the floor. Devon stood back wondering what the fuck was going on. "You're cheating on me with a fuckin' man?"

"Do what nih? Oh, bitch I know you've lost your fuckin' mind. That's one of my damn clients. If you would've allowed me to explain before you snatched the fuckin' phone out of my hand, then you would have known that."

Reginald sat on the phone laughing. Devon didn't find anything to be funny. He stood there as if he were really upset with Keyanna, but he wasn't. He was actually retracing the past few days in his mind to see what he could've said, or did that implied that he may have cheated on her. He'd never seen Keyanna act so insecure, and it bothered him. Yeah, he was wrong for stepping out on their marriage, but he could've sworn that he'd been careful with hiding his indiscretions.

"Oh, my God. I'm so sorry. I didn't mean to a—"

Devon cut her off. "You never mean to. I don't know what's gotten into your ass lately, but I'm sick of it. You keep accusing me of cheating, and you've been acting all violent and shit. I don't like that bullshit, nor did I sign up for it," Devon scolded Keyanna. He could see the tears in her eyes, and it saddened him. He didn't like to see her hurt, but he was tired of the way she was acting.

"I said I was sorry."

"You always saying you're sorry, but you keep doing the same shit over and over again. I'm tired of it, Keyanna. Either you're going to straighten up and act like you trust me or we can go right on down to the courthouse and end this shit."

"Let's talk about this when you get off the phone."

"No, you didn't want to wait earlier until I got off the phone to talk, so now there's no need to wait until I end the call. As a matter fact, get out of my way." Devon picked his phone up off the floor. "I'll be leaving Memphis in a couple of hours. We can talk then," he told Reginald and ended the call.

"Where are you going?" Keyanna questioned Devon. He walked out the bathroom, still naked, and she chased right behind him. They found themselves in the middle of the hallway, arguing.

"I'm getting the fuck away from you and your crazy ass friends. I don't want this shit anymore, Keyanna."

"Baby, I said I was sorry. I've been going through some shit since I had the baby. I'm depressed because I can't please you, and it makes me feel like you're getting it from somewhere else. You can't blame me for the way I've been acting. Depression is a disease."

"Fuck you and your depression, Keyanna. I know your ass is lying because everything was fine until we talked about coming up here. Porscha is the only disease in your fuckin' life."

Suddenly, Porscha's room door flew open. Keyanna and Devon were still standing in the hallway naked. Neither of them cared. Besides, it wasn't like she hadn't seen them both naked before.

"Why did I hear my name?" Porscha quizzed.

"Mind your fuckin' business, bitch!" Devon roared.

"Aye, you not about to be disrespecting my wife like that!" Michael joined them all in the hallway.

"Nigga, fuck you too." Devon was amped up. He was so pissed at all of them that he was willing to knock the fuck out of either one of them at any given moment.

"Porscha and Michael, I appreciate y'all trying to help me, but this has nothing to do with either of y'all. I fucked up, and I have to fix this on my own," Keyanna owned up to her fault in the situation.

"I wasn't helping anybody. I just wanted to know why I heard my name in an argument that had nothing to do with me," Porscha chided.

"It has everything to do with you. As long as Keyanna is nowhere near you and your fuckin' drama, she's the woman that I met and fell in love with. Every time she's around you, some bullshit goes down. Who the fuck would even want a friend that was always in some shit? I would've stopped fuckin' with you a long time ago," Devon announced.

"Well, you didn't," Porscha stated and walked toward Devon. Michael pulled her back. Neither Michael nor Keyanna caught on to what was just said. That was how Devon knew that everyone standing there was heated.

"This shit has gotten way out of hand. Y'all need to put some fuckin' clothes on so we can sit down and talk," Michael requested.

"No, he's right. I should've walked away a long time ago," Keyanna acknowledged. Everyone looked at her, wondering what she was talking about. The way she made her last statement left things up in the air about which relationship she should've walked away from.

Devon watched as Keyanna walked inside the bedroom they'd been sleeping in. He glanced back at Michael and Porscha and shook his head before going after Keyanna. When he entered the room, he heard her on the phone getting a rental car. It took him a minute to realize she was packing whatever belonged to her and DJ. When Keyanna hung the phone up, she checked on DJ, grabbed some clothes, and waltzed back out of the room. She went back to the bathroom so she could clean herself up and get dressed. Devon noticed her phone lying on the bed. He picked it up and scrolled through it.

Devon found that Keyanna had booked a hotel and rental car. She wasn't going to Mississippi, but to Georgia. He went through her emails and came across one that she'd just sent to her attorney asking to get her divorce papers together. When he said she needed to walk away from a relationship, he meant the one she had with Porscha, not the one she had with him. What the fuck was he going to do now?

### *Chapter Twenty-Two:*

Keyanna hated the way she'd lost her best friend and husband at the same damn time. She didn't understand any of it and wasn't about to question God about it. She took it as negativity being removed from her life. Somebody else had to do it because she would've never been brave enough to do it on her own.

After taking a quick shower and brushing her teeth, she threw her clothes on and walked back to the guest room. Devon was standing over the bed, unpacking everything that she'd previously packed. She was fully aware that he was doing that because he wanted her to say something to him, but she wasn't going to say shit. She checked on DJ and moved around Devon as if he weren't there. She began putting everything back in their bags.

"What the fuck are you doing, Keyanna?" Devon broke the silence that was between them.

"What does it look like I'm doing? I'm leaving. You were right when you said that things had to change and what you didn't sign up for. I didn't sign up for this shit either."

"Come on, Key. I was just mad. You know I don't want our marriage to end."

"Is that what it was, or you know that as soon as we sign those papers, I'll be getting half of everything, child support, and alimony out of your ass?" She threw out shit to him that he hadn't even thought about.

"Baby, I was upset because of the way you acted with a client on the phone."

"Devon, I'm not stupid. I know that wasn't a fuckin' client. Your ass was up to something... Just admit it!" She stopped long enough to focus her attention on him. Devon didn't say shit; there really wasn't shit for him to say.

"I fucked up, Keyanna. I cheated on you," Devon admitted. Keyanna dropped what was in her hand and just stared at him.

"Tell me something I don't know. Then, I saw where you scheduled to have a vasectomy done, and you weren't even going to tell me."

"How the fuck did you find out about that?"

"I guess you forgot that our calendars sync so we would always know what each other had going on. Anything you put in yours, I can see. You forgot about that, huh?" Devon couldn't say shit. "I'm glad that you weren't trying to lie your way out of that. Especially, knowing that I have proof of it. I should've allowed you to go through with it and used that as the main ground for our divorce."

"I don't want a divorce!" Devon raised his voice at her. Keyanna's eyebrows flew up, and she threw her hands on her hips.

"I'm sorry, but who the fuck are you yelling at?"

"I wasn't yelling. I'm telling you from my heart that I love you. I fucked up that one time, and I have never done it again. I've went out of my way trying to make things right."

"Including trying to hide it?" She pointed out.

"Yeah, I was wrong. I should've came clean right when it happened, but I didn't. I'm sorry, Key. I didn't mean to hurt you. I was going through my own problems then. Please, don't do this. Don't leave me." Keyanna glanced up at Devon and could see tears in his eyes. She hadn't seen those since their wedding. "Let me make this right," he pleaded with her.

"I need time to myself."

"You can't take my son," he barked.

"You mean the son you never wanted? The son you'll let holler because you don't want to deal with him? The same son you walk past as if he never existed?" Sadness washed over Devon's face, but he didn't say a word. "You think I couldn't see the way you were treating him? I understand that you didn't want a child, but he's here. Besides, it wasn't like we were doing anything to prevent the shit."

"You're right. I fucked up all the way around. Please let me find a way to correct my wrongs. Baby, I swear to you that I can fix it. We can go to counseling."

"It's crazy that when you were all big and bad, you had no problems threatening me with a divorce, but as soon as I say okay, then you want to make like you're hurt. Don't be hurt about it. You need to have the same energy you had with those threats when it comes down to signing these divorce papers," Keyanna commented.

Keyanna was not ready for what Devon did next. He dropped down to the floor like the rat looking dude from Jodeci and hit that Keith Sweat beg.

"Please, baby, baby, please!" he pleaded with her again. Keyanna tried her best to keep her composure, but she couldn't. She had to laugh because the shit was hilarious.

"Get up," she instructed him when she was finally able to stop laughing.

"I'm serious, Keyanna. I can't envision my life without you," Devon honestly spoke.

"Yet, it was okay for you to try to walk away from me? Oh, now I get it. As long as you can leave it's cool, but if a bitch try to leave you, that's a problem. This ain't no competition."

"I never said it was. I was mad when I said what I said. I didn't mean it."

"Well." *(clap)* "You." *(clap)* "Never." *(clap)* "Should." *(clap)* "Have." *(clap)* "Said." *(clap)* "What." *(clap)* "You." *(clap)* "Said." *(clap)*

Keyanna continued to talk to Devon, clapping between each word to let him know that she meant business. She wasn't about to be his damn toy. He wasn't gonna put her on a shelf and pull her down whenever he felt like it. His ass spoke to her like he was her father and she was on punishment. The worst part of it all was that he did it in front of Porscha and Michael. She was determined to teach his ass a lesson, even if it meant leaving him for good. He was going to respect and appreciate her one way or another.

### *Chapter Twenty-Three:*

Porscha stepped back inside of her room, grinning on the inside at the fact that it could very well be the end of things for Keyanna and Devon. That was right up her alley because that meant that she could leave Michael and her and Devon could finally be together.

"You ready to go?" Michael asked her.

"Go where?" She looked at him with a state of confusion.

"To the damn hotel."

"I ain't goin' to no hotel so they can tear our shit up," Porscha snapped.

"Girl, ain't nobody about to tear up this damn house, and even if they did, this shit is material, and we can always get another one."

"Is that so?" Porscha inquired, she looked at him sideways because she was doing the best she could to bite her tongue about what she'd found on him.

"What is that supposed to mean? You know like I know that we have more than enough money to get any and everything that we want," Michael called himself assuring her.

"Just get ready. I need to call the hotel and get everything together. I got sidetracked while they were doing all that hollering and shit," she told him.

Porscha got on the phone and booked a room at the DoubleTree. She made a few requests for some things she wanted done to her room and let them go ahead and charge the card to the bank account she had of her own that Michael was not aware of.

Porscha packed her an overnight bag and rushed to slide the paperwork she'd made copies of inside of her bag so that Michael wouldn't see them.

"Michaelllllll..." she called out to him after she'd gone inside the bathroom to gather her hygiene items.

"What's up?" He appeared in front of the door. He'd changed out of his work clothes and now wore a pair of basketball shorts and a white tee.

"Where you going with those on?" Porscha asked him.

"What you mean?"

"Don't fuckin' play stupid with me. You know damn well that your ass don't walk out the door in no damn basketball shorts or grey sweatpants. You trying to get a bitch fucked up, aren't you?"

Michael walked away shaking his head. Porscha picked up the items that she'd gone in the bathroom after and marched inside the room behind Michael.

"So you don't hear me talking to you?"

"Porscha, I'm about to be with you, so who's going to be looking at me in some damn basketball shorts. Plus, we both know that don't nobody want my ass."

"You tell that shit to someone else and see if they believe it. I'll never believe no bullshit like that," she told him. "Anyways, I need to go pick up a few other items, and I'll meet you at the hotel." She gave him the information to the hotel and grabbed her bags. Porscha softly kissed Michael on his lips before leaving out of the room. She passed by the room that Keyanna and Devon were inside of. She could still hear them fussing and that made her feel good. That was until she heard Devon begging Keyanna not to leave him.

Porscha kicked the door a few times and took off running toward the front door. She kept running until she was safely inside of her car. She really wished it was Devon's ass that she was kicking because she felt played. There was no reason for him to be begging Keyanna to stay with him when he and Porscha had discussed them being together on more than one occasion.

Porscha had just crank her car up when she saw Keyanna come strolling out of the house with a few suitcases. Porscha stayed put until she saw if Devon walked out the door behind her.

"What the fuck are you looking at?" Porscha heard Keyanna yell.

"Who you talking to?" Porscha jumped out of her car and stormed toward Keyanna. Keyanna threw everything that was in her hands in the trunk of their SUV and turned to face Porscha.

"I'm talking to you. You the one looking at me like there's a problem or something. If you got something that you want to say to me, then you need to say it."

Porscha and Keyanna stood in an intense stare down for what seemed like forever. Michael came trampling outside to see what all the commotion was about, but he never said a word. Devon was right behind him. Porscha was sure that as loud as they were talking, it wouldn't be long before other people in their neighborhood came out to see what was going on as well.

"Key, what are we doing? This isn't us. We've had fights before, but nothing compared to this. You're my sister, and I love you," Porscha somewhat lied. But there was no way she was going to tell Keyanna that she wanted her life. Keyanna was a force to be reckoned with when she was mad.

Keyanna stood before Porscha for a few more minutes before she finally said, "Let me tell you something. If you go down that street, take about two rights and a left, you'll see where you had me fucked up at. Keep that fake shit over there," she sassed and turned to leave. Porscha grabbed her shoulder and turned her back around.

"I'm serious, Keyanna. I love you. I was wrong for the way I tripped on you. I had a lot of anger pinned up inside of me, and

I took it out on you. Come on, sis. You can't be that mad at me."

"I just need some time to think. I don't like the way none of this shit went down. I haven't had drama in my life in forever, and I'm not about to start having any now. Something has to change," Keyanna announced before yanking her arm away from Porscha and heading back inside the house. After a few minutes, she came back out with a diaper bag and DJ, strapped in his car seat. Once he was safely strapped inside the car, she got inside and sped away. Devon was still out there practically begging her not to leave him.

"This some bullshit. It's all your fault!" Devon yelled at Porscha.

"Exactly how the hell is this my fault? You're the one that pissed her off. Shit, y'all were arguing before I ever said anything to either of y'all. The only reason I ever said anything in the first place was because I heard my name being mentioned."

"Baby, you don't have to explain shit to this dude. Go do what you were going to do, and I'll meet you at the hotel. They can handle their own problems. I'm trynna put this banana in your monkey; that's all you need to be worried about," Michael chimed in.

"What the fuck are you going to a hotel with this chump for?" Devon asked out of the blue. Porscha stood frozen because she didn't know what to say or do. It was only a matter of time before her and Devon's secret came out, but she was hoping it would be after she served Michael with divorce papers.

"Why are you questioning my wife about what she's going to do? I'm her fuckin' husband, not you," Michael growled.

"I'm not talking to you; I'm talking to Porscha. Now, answer me, dammit" Devon roared.

"Huh? I didn't hear what you said," Porscha played dumb.

"I know I'm not talking fast, so you must be listening slow. Clean that fuckin' gunk out of your mufuckin' ears and answer me." Devon jerked Porscha up, damn near breaking her arm.

"Please, don't do this. You're about to let him know what's been going on between us. You're supposed to be going after your wife, not going back and forth with me," Porscha whispered to him. Neither of them was paying attention to what Michael was doing. Therefore, they were unprepared for what happened next.

Michael ran full speed ahead toward Devon. Devon saw him out the corner of his eyes, and he jumped out the way, causing Michael to run into Porscha. Upon impact, the back of Porscha's head hit the ground. Michael and Devon engaged in a full out fist fight, not realizing what had happened with Porscha. It wasn't until a neighbor came running over yelling for help that the two men stopped. Michael ran over to where Porscha was as Devon stood back to see what was going on. Porscha stayed conscious for as long as she could, but when the darkness fell upon her, there was nothing more she could do.

### *Chapter Twenty-Four:*

Keyanna rode around Memphis while DJ peacefully slept in his car seat. She didn't know where she was going and had no one else to call that lived there. It would've been wise for her to find a hotel or better yet, go back to Porscha's house to try to make things between them better. But, she wasn't ready. Whatever was going on between her and Porscha would have to be worked out when she had the energy for it.

Keyanna's phone rang continuously as she drove. She knew that it was nobody but Devon calling, so she didn't answer. She didn't want to say anything that she'd potentially regret later, and she really didn't want to hear his voice. There was nothing she could say to him to change the events of the day or her thoughts of wanting to get a divorce. Something was off about their relationship, and she'd given up on trying to figure out what it was.

Abruptly, Keyanna pulled over to the side of the road. Tears relentlessly ran down her face. She punched the steering wheel twice before yelling, "Whyyyy?" The moment she heard DJ moving around in his seat, she stopped yelling and looked back at him. He must've gotten comfortable because he stopped moving with his eyes remained closed. She laughed because the way he was lying there, you would've thought he'd just gotten done doing something extraneous. She removed her phone from the center console and decided to call one of her other friends, Shana.

Shana and Keyanna met when she went to an interview at the law office that she was working part-time for. They exchanged numbers once Keyanna got the job so that Shana could assist her whenever she needed help. Through their many conversations, Keyanna and Shana grew a bond, and they became accustomed to talking to each other, each and every day. More than Keyanna had talked to Porscha in a long time. That was the very reason she didn't have a problem with walking away from her relationship with Porscha. Yeah, they'd been friends for as long as she could remember, but their relationship was toxic at times. It took motherhood to show her what she really needed in her life. Neither drama or stress were included in that need.

"Hey, boo," Shana sang through the phone.

"Hey, chick. What's up with you?"

"Nothing really. Sitting around here trying to get a little laundry done so I can get dinner started," Shana replied.

"Oh okay. You need me to call you back?"

"No, ma'am. I'm good. What's going on? You sound down?"

"There's so much shit that's happened since I've been here that I don't believe half of it myself."

"What you mean?" Shana questioned. Keyanna heard the concern in her voice. She must've stopped what she was doing because Keyanna no longer heard movement on the other end of the phone.

Keyanna was still pulled over on the side of the road. Cars zoomed past her like she wasn't even there. Then, there were a few cars that stopped to see if she was okay. She practically shooed them away because she didn't want people she didn't know all in her business.

"Key, you there?" Shana's voice boomed through the phone.

"Uh... Yeah... Yeah... I'm good. You good?" Keyanna was so out of it that she started to get confused and started stuttering over her words.

"Keyanna, I don't know what's going on with you, but you have me scared. Are you okay? Do I need to come up there?"

"No, I'm fine. Devon and I got into it. It's crazy because we've never had a big blowout fight like we did today."

"What? What happened? That's not like you guys at all," Shana implied.

"To make a long story short, Porscha walked in on me sucking Devon's dick. She got mad and stormed out of the room. But even before that, she had been throwing shade since the time I walked through her front door. I don't know what's going on with her or who she's become, but she's not the same Porscha that I looked at as my sister; she's evil. She's a monster," Keyanna pointed out.

"She may be a monster, but you're the fuckin' slayer. Don't let her or anyone else steal your joy. I don't know why she would get mad at you for suckin' your dick," Shana announced.

"My dick?" Keyanna probed.

"You fuckin' right. Your nigga, your dick." Shana laughed. Keyanna knew she was only trying to make light of the situation, but nothing helped. Keyanna was furious at the way that Porscha had been acting, but Devon made matters ten times worse with his smart-ass mouth and hollering.

"What did Devon do to you?" Shana tried to get down to the nitty gritty. Keyanna liked that about her. She always went past the small talk and was ready to get down to business.

"It's a long story. At the end of the day, just know that what he did is almost unforgivable."

Keyanna didn't want to tell Shana everything that had happened between her and Devon. She was a firm believer in keeping family and friends out of your business. Reason being, if she decided to stay with him, she didn't want the people closest to her judging him or treating him any differently.

"Well, I have nothing but time on my hands. Spill it!"

Keyanna deliberated over what she wanted to do. She was not about to tell Shana too much, no matter how much she felt she'd feel better after letting it all out. She opened her mouth to speak but was cut off.

"Hold on," Shana told her and clicked over.

"Thank God!" Keyanna sighed. She was relieved that someone had called Shana. That was a sign to her that she needed to stick to her original plan and keep the information about her relationship to herself.

While she waited for Shana to come back on the line, Devon called in. She was mad at him, but she still loved him. She loved him enough to walk away from him, but she didn't want to leave him having to worry if her and their son was okay.

"Key?" Shana came back on the line right as Keyanna decided to answer Devon's call.

"I'm here," Keyanna informed her. She was about to tell her to hold on so she could answer Devon's call, but he'd already hung up.

"Sorry about that, that was my mother. She needs me to come pick my daughter up early. Are you going to be okay?" Shana sincerely asked.

"I'll be fine. Thanks for the talk," Keyanna replied. She was thankful that Shana came back on the line when she did because she felt that talking to Devon would've made him think that she was giving in and she didn't want that.

"Anytime, sis. I'll call you back later to check on you. Don't be over there stressing either; things will work themselves out. I promise," Shana assured her. That made her feel a little better, but not enough to make her return to Porscha's house.

Right when Keyanna had hung up the phone from talking to Shana, there was an incoming call from Michael. All types of thoughts plagued her mind as she pondered over why he could be calling her. It hit her that maybe Devon could be using Michael's phone to reach out to her. After a few brief moments of wondering why she was getting a call from Michaels' phone, she decided to go ahead and answer.

"What?" she yelled through the phone as soon as she answered.

"Get to the hospital right now," Michael hollered.

"Why? What's going on? Is it Devon?" Keyanna's nerves went from zero to a thousand real quick.

"Keyanna, calm down. I need you to get to the hospital." Michael hung up the phone without giving her a chance to respond. She was a nervous wreck and wanted to know what the hell was going on. Had Michael tried to kill Devon? Had they gotten into another fight after she left? She was confused and didn't know what to do. Then the fact that Michael told her to get to the hospital without telling her which hospital, knowing she didn't know much about Memphis, didn't make anything any better for her.

Keyanna looked up hospitals on her phone. She entered the address in her GPS to the first hospital that popped up and moved her car back onto the road. If she had to drive to every hospital in Memphis to get to her husband, then she was going to do it. She was angry at herself for the problems that her and Devon were having. Everything was fine before they left Mississippi, and she wished they would've stayed that way.

With her car in motion, she received a text. It was from Michael telling her which hospital they were at. She quickly switched the information in her GPS and made a U-turn to head toward Baptist-Memorial Hospital.

### *Chapter Twenty-Five:*

Michael rode in the ambulance with Porscha. He couldn't believe what had transpired at their home. That was the second time in a matter of days that the police showed up at his home. He had a gut feeling that the home owners' association was going to want them to move for bringing that ratchetness to their quiet neighborhood.

On their way to the hospital he texted Keyanna to let her know what hospital they were headed to. She was mad at Porscha at the moment, but with all of their fights, Michael figured it was only temporary. So, there was really no reason for her to not be there when Porscha needed her. By the time the ambulance made it to the hospital, Porscha was still out like a light.

"Is she going to be alright?" Michael asked the paramedics as they were rolling her off the ambulance.

"Sir, you'd have to ask the doctor that." Michael was told. He didn't like that answer, so he jumped off the ambulance and ran on inside. He began looking for anyone he thought could help. He ended up running into Keyanna who was there holding a hollering DJ.

"What the fuck happened?" Keyanna interrogated him.

"Ask your lame ass husband," Michael hissed.

"What exactly does Devon have to do with this?"

"Stop asking me all of those fuckin' questions and ask his punk ass. This is not the first time he caused a fight at my house, but I can guarantee you that it will be the last." By the time Michael finished his statement, Devon came jogging into the hospital.

"How the fuck did you get here? I know you ain't get yo' ass in one of my vehicles," Michael fussed.

"Nigga, you worried about a damn car when your wife could be back there about to die," Devon replied. Michael turned around as Porscha was being wheeled inside the hospital. He followed the stretcher's every move. He wanted to know what was going on with his wife and why she was unresponsive.

"We need you to wait out here, sir," the hospital staff told Michael. They pushed Porscha inside a room and shut the door and curtains behind them.

Michael hysterically waited in front of the room. He paced back and forth so much, he could've plowed a hole in the floor with his hard ass shoes. Several people walked up to him and tried to get him to have a seat in the waiting area, but he refused; he was not leaving Porscha's side for anybody.

The doctor came out of the room roughly thirty minutes later. Michael went over to him so fast, the doctor stepped to the side. Michael was sure the doctor thought he was going to run him over, but that wasn't the case. All he wanted to do was make sure his wife was good.

"Are you Mr. Alexander?"

"Yes, I am. How is she, Doc? Is she talking? Is she going to be okay?" Michael asked the doctor so many questions without giving him the chance to answer any of them. "Are you going to answer me, Doc?"

"Are you going to give me the chance to?" Michael clamped his mouth together and shook his head to give the doctor a chance to speak.

"Now, my name is Dr. Spann. I'm the emergency room doctor that has been working on your wife and will be looking after her while she is in the emergency room. She had a pretty hard fall. Do you mind me asking what happened?"

"Yes, I do mind. What the fuck does what happened have to do with you treating her? Come on, Doc. Stop with all the bullshit and get straight to the point. What the fuck is up with my wife?"

The doctor looked around the waiting room. Michael already knew what was up.

"I'm sorry for talking to you like that. I'm just scared."

"As you should be. She hit the ground hard and has a concussion. We are going to admit her and keep her overnight so we can run some more tests on her. But, she's going to be fine."

"Thank you, Doc. Thank you so much." Michael grabbed the doctor's hands and relentlessly shook it.

Dr. Spann leaned in to Michael so he could talk more personally with him. "I understand she is your wife, but I don't tolerate abuse. Not on my watch. If I sense that something fishy is going on, I will call the police and have you hauled out of here," he informed Michael. Michael got scared all over again. He never would've thought anyone would see him as the type of man that would beat his wife. He had to clear his name.

"I promise you that I didn't put my hands on her. Her best friend's husband and I got to fighting and Porscha was hit in the process. I would never lay a finger on my wife," Michael sincerely insisted. "I love her with every fiber of my being," he added.

"Good, because no woman deserves to be hit by a man. Now, you can go see her, but you have to promise me not to do anything that will cause her any stress. We want her to get better," Dr. Spann asserted in a stern tone.

"I understand. Thanks again." Michael gradually walked over to the door. His palms instantly became sweaty, and his body started to feel hot. He thought that he should've asked the doctor if Porscha was up before he went in there. However, Dr. Spann stopped him right as he had put his hand on the door handle.

"Oh, before I forget, Mr. Alexander." Michael turned to give Dr. Spann his full attention.

"Yes?" Michael answered.

"Congratulations..." Michael stood still waiting for Dr. Spann to tell him what he was talking about. "You don't know, do you?"

"Know what?"

"Your wife is pregnant," Dr. Spann informed him. He trolled away from Michael without allowing him to get a word in. Michael could've passed out because he didn't know how Porscha would react to the news. She had a miscarriage not too long ago and vowed that she wasn't going to have any more kids, any time soon.

Michael suddenly dreaded stepping inside the room with Porscha. Her eyes were wide open, and she immediately rolled them when she saw him. Michael took a seat in the chair next to the bed and didn't open his mouth. The news of her being pregnant was just going to have to wait until some other time.

### *Chapter Twenty-Six:*

"Why are you here?" Porscha asked Michael once he stepped inside her room. She watched his every move as he maneuvered toward her bed. He took a seat in the chair next to her bed and grabbed ahold of her hand.

"You know that I wasn't going to leave your side," Michael commented.

"You're the reason that I'm even in here," she muttered. "So I don't see the need for you to be here," she added and snatched her hand away from him.

"I know and I'm sor—" Michael stopped himself. "Why the hell is it that you are so quick to pounce on me and let Devon get away with everything? What the fuck is up with that?"

"I'm not letting him get away with shit. He's not my husband, you are, and you should know better. Everything that has happened since their visit has always had something to do with you."

"Do you really think I would've allowed them to come here if I knew all of this shit was going to happen? I was only trying to look out for you, my wife!" he emphasized. "Yet, you are so ready to condemn me without considering how much I was really trying to make sure you were good."

"I didn't condemn you and I sure as hell didn't need you worrying about me. Shit, it wasn't like you cared enough to listen to me when I wanted to tell you what all of my dreams were about. That's when you really should've been there for me, but you weren't. Instead, you wanted to bring other people in to be here for me when my own damn husband couldn't be. I married you, not them."

"I was only trying to fix shit," Michael barked.

"Fix shit? Michael, I'm not broken so there ain't a damn thing you can fix," Porscha snapped. "And when the fuck was you going to tell me that we were broke?" Porscha hollered. The color drained from Michael's face like he'd seen a ghost. It wasn't the right time for them to be having that conversation, but after everything that transpired, there was no way Porscha could hold her feelings in any longer.

"W-w-w-what did you just say?" he stuttered.

"You heard everything that I said. Why the hell didn't you tell me that we didn't have any more money? You allowed me to walk around spending money that we didn't have like everything was okay, only for me to end up being embarrassed in front of my best friend and the woman from the church. I had to cuss that bitch out. Do you have any idea how that made me feel? Hell, do you even care? I never thought I'd ever have to say that we were broke." She paused. "Nigga, we Broke *BROKE*," Porscha added.

"We aren't really broke. I'm working on some projects that are going to give us more money than we could've ever imagined."

"Is that so?"

"Yes, and if you would've asked me about it instead of going through my shit, like I was dumb and wouldn't notice it, then you would know," Michael chided.

"Ask you about it? I shouldn't have had to ask you about shit. You should've been willing to tell me the truth from the jump. It's not fair to me that I even had to start my own investigation against my husband. All of that just shows me that I can't trust you. I can't even trust you to protect me."

"Porscha, I've protected you from everything, ever since we got married. I've had your back, even when your ass has been dead ass wrong. Hell, I even apologize to you and allow you to get away with bullshit that I wouldn't dare allow the next mufucka to get away with," Michael quipped.

"I'm your fuckin' wife; you're supposed to do that shit. What the fuck you think this is?" Porscha sat up in the bed and raised the back of it up so she could relax her back against it.

"I know... I know... I was hoping to correct the issue myself. It wasn't like I was doing anything to hurt you."

"If you knew better, you would've done better. This relationship is really over, Michael. I've been unhappy for a while, and this little stunt you pulled with not paying the bills and shit has only made matters worse."

"What are you saying?" Michael stood from his chair. He stared into Porscha's eyes.

"I'm saying that I want a divorce. I was unhappy before, but like I said, all the shit that took place recently and the lies are unforgivable. My company is on the line because of the lack of funding. What am I goi—"

"Shut up!" Michael cut her off. "Everything is me or I. What the fuck happened to we and us? You didn't marry your damn self, and it seems to me that the only reason you even married me was because of what I could do for you."

As Michael went on and on, calling himself putting Porscha in her place, she couldn't do anything but take in everything that he was saying. He could call her a gold-digger or whatever he wanted to call him, but she did have love for him at one point. Somehow that love drifted away over time. It didn't help that what she had with Devon was only supposed to be a fling until they got comfortable with each other and she caught feelings. She'd never be able to explain to Keyanna, Michael, or anyone else how she ended up catching feelings for her best friend's husband.

"Michael, would you listen for once in your life?" Porscha had heard enough. She wanted Michael to shut up and give her the floor.

"No, I won't listen. All I've been doing is listening to you talk crazy to me and treat me like Geoffrey the fuckin' butler instead of Michael, your gotdamn husband. You think I don't see how you be looking at other niggas with those 'come fuck me eyes'?

You think I don't know that you be texting some other nigga when you aren't around me? Hell, some of those messages was when your cockeyed ass was laid in the bed next to me. Yeah, I've seen all of that, and I let that shit slide because I felt like you were wrestling with your own personal demons. At the end of the day, I have fuckin' feelings too. If you want a divorce, then please know that you won't get a damn dime from me. I may have lied, but I never cheated. Shit, because of your infidelity, I need to be contacting my attorney now to see what the fuck I can get out of this shit."

Porscha shut down because she didn't think that Michael knew about what she'd been doing behind his back. Devon wasn't the only man that she fooled with, and he probably wasn't going to be the last. However, he was the only one that she found herself loving outside of Michael. The one thing she was glad about out of everything that Michael had said to her was the fact that he didn't know that Devon was one of the men that she was messing around with and if he did, he did a damn good job not mentioning it. *Could he be keeping it to himself to blackmail me for it later?* She asked herself.

"You don't have shit to say now?"

"Michael, I want you to get out. You only came in here trying to flip shit on me because you were in the wrong. Yeah, I may have talked to other men, but I haven't fucked any of them," she lied.

"You really expect me to believe that?" Michael chirped.

"You can believe what you want to believe; I know who and what has been inside of this pussy," she replied. Michael started patting himself down in search of something. When he found his cell phone in his back pocket, he pulled it out. *Awe hell,* Porscha thought to herself.

"Rico: Damn girl, I wish I could put your pussy in my pocket so I could pull it out and fuck you whenever I felt like it. Desmond: Are you in the giving mood for the holiday cuz a nigga in need of some fiya head? Lucci: Come ride this dick, girl; you don't even need a seatbelt. Swisher: You need to put that pussy on my taste buds. Guru: Yo—"

"Stop it," she interrupted him. "You don't have to read all that shit back to me. I'm certain I've read it all before." Porscha had to stop herself from smiling at the thought of all the wonderful sex sessions and conversations she had with those men.

"There were over twenty damn men, Porscha. Don't you care that you out there giving out more cat than a fuckin' Chinese restaurant?"

"Just because you saw those messages doesn't mean that I actually slept with them. Why couldn't they just be texting me and trying to entice me to cheat on my husband?"

"You got a mirror?" Michael randomly asked.

"A mirror for what?" Porscha pondered over why the fuck he'd ask for something so dumb and random at a time like this.

"I need to see if I got 'stupid' written on my forehead or some shit cuz you trying it right now. You trying to play me like I have a mental retardation diagnosis or some shit."

"Michael, please leave. I don't have time for this shit. I heard the doctor tell you that I didn't need any stress and you brought your *Willy Wonka in the Chocolate Factory* looking ass in here starting shit."

"I ain't started nothing. I came in here to check on you and you trying to make me look dumb; you need to find you somebody else to play with," Michael barked.

"If you get the fuck out, then I might be able to find somebody else to play with," Porscha snapped back.

If you would've told Porscha that her marriage would've ended the way that it appeared to be on the verge of, she never would've believed you. When she found that information on Michael, she wanted to deliver it to him in such a way that he'd regret the day that he ever lied to her. What she never expected was for him to reveal all of the information that he had against her. She thought for sure that she'd done a better job at covering her tracks.

"Leave!" Porscha yelled and pointed at the door.

"Fine, I'm going to let Keyanna know that she can come see you. I'll be back later; this conversation is nowhere near over," he assured her. Porscha rolled her eyes and watched as he exited the room.

Porscha didn't understand why Keyanna was even there when she'd just got into it with her. They'd gotten into it plenty of times before, but it was nothing like what they'd experienced today. Porscha had nightmares about what was going on in her marriage that she never even realized. She wished she could close her eyes and everything that she was feeling and going through at the moment would all be a part of the nightmare and when she woke up, things would be back to normal. It was a bit far stretch, but she was willing to try it. She closed her eyes and hoped for the best. When she opened them and saw that she was still inside the hospital bed, she wondered what could happen next.

### *Chapter Twenty-Seven:*

Keyanna sat in the waiting area to hear from Michael. She saw Devon sitting across the way, staring at her. She wanted to punch both of his eyes shut so he wouldn't be able to look at her any further.

"Are you ready to talk to me?" Devon asked her from across the room.

"If I was, then I would've been said something to your ass," Keyanna responded, rolling her eyes.

"I really wish you'd stop acting like that. This isn't even you."

"And how the fuck would you know? You've been too busy concentrating on the next bitch to know what I have going on with me," she sassed to him.

"It was only one bitch," he quickly replied.

"Oh, because it was just one bitch, that's supposed to make the shit okay?"

"Ssssshhhhh... Y'all are going to have to simmer down or I'm going to have to ask you to leave," a security guard told them.

"Don't shush me. I'll talk as loud as I want to, and you not putting me out of shit until I find out what's wrong with my friend," Keyanna snapped. She stood and had her finger pointing in the man's face.

"Keyanna..." She heard Michael say her name. She turned around and jogged toward him. She threw her arms around his neck and embraced him. She didn't give a damn how Devon felt about seeing her hug his enemy. The only reason she hugged him was because she felt if anything bad had happened to Porscha, then Michael wouldn't have come out so calm.

"How is she?"

"Come over here," Michael told her. He looked up at Devon then turned his back toward him. "She's fine. She has a concussion, so they are going to keep her overnight to run a few more tests on her."

"What happened, Michael? How did she end up here? Did you hit her?" Keyanna glared into his eyes and questioned him.

"No, I would never hit her or any other woman. How is it so easy for people to peg me as a woman beater?"

"It's not about pegging you as anything. You'd be surprised at the men who hit their women; it be the ones you never expect to do it."

"Whatever. I'm not that guy," Michael insisted.

"Well, just tell me what happened," Keyanna requested again, putting a hand on Michael's shoulder while he placed one of his hands around her waist.

"After you left, Devon called himself checking her and telling her that all of this was her fault."

"All of what?"

"This shit between you and him basically," Michael broke down to her. "It was bad. Of course, you know she was going to go toe-to-toe with his ass, and I wasn't about to stand back and watch the shit go down like that, so I stepped up to defend my wife. Devon was talking so much shit that I ran up on him, but he moved out the way, and I ended up knocking Porcha down. That's how she hit her head. I'd never put my hands on her, and you of all people should know that," Michael explained.

"You can take your hands off my wife now." Keyanna quickly removed her hand from Michael's shoulder when she heard Devon's voice. Michael left his hand in the same spot around her waist and smirked at the fact that he was getting under Devon's skin.

"Don't start nothing in this hospital," she told him.

"I'm not starting shit, but I don't like the way this nigga putting his hands all over you. If he wants to touch somebody, he needs to be in there touching on his wife."

"Please, don't do this here," Keyanna pleaded with Devon.

"I'll not do this when this mufucka take his cornball ass fingers from around your mufuckin' waist," Devon spat.

"Fine. It ain't even that serious," Michael commented and removed his hand.

"Can I see her?" Keyanna asked Michael, trying to change the subject back to the real reason they were even there.

"Yes, but the doctor said she don't need any stress." Keyanna noticed Michael drop his head so she pondered over what he wasn't telling her. She didn't want to cause any more problems, so she debated over whether she really needed to go in and see her or not.

"Maybe I should wait and see her some other time."

"No, she needs you. She's being a bitch to me because she blames me for this like everyone else is doing. Go to her, please." Keyanna heard the sadness in Michael's voice and could see a depressed expression on his face.

"Is everything okay? I know we don't always get along, but I do care," Keyanna expressed.

"It's fine. I'm going to get an Uber home to get her an overnight bag and I'll be back. Don't leave her alone," Michael requested.

"I got you," Keyanna assured him. "Here, watch your son or is that too much to ask?" she stated to Devon who was standing over her and Michael like a fire breathing dragon.

"Yeah, whatever," he told her. He reached out like he was about to snatch DJ up, but when he saw the look on her face, he softened his motions. Keyanna didn't leave the waiting area to follow Michael to Porscha's room until she saw Devon sit down with DJ. When Michael showed her where they were keeping Porscha until they moved her to her actual room, he left. Not before Keyanna told him that she would text him and let him know her room number if they happened to move her before he got back.

Keyanna stood outside of Porscha's room and deliberated over whether or not she really could deal with Porscha and her attitude. She was her best friend. Her sister. But, she changed. Porscha hadn't been the same person that she'd grown to love as family over the years.

"You might as well come on in; I can see your shoes under the curtain," Porscha called out. Taking her time, Keyanna opened the door. "Have a seat," Porscha directed, pointing at the seat that was next to her hospital bed.

"How are you feeling?" Keyanna asked, still standing by the door. She figured she'd wait to see how things went with their conversation before she actually got comfortable enough to sit next to Porscha's crazy ass. She didn't want to put herself in a position where Porscha could get mad and try to choke her ass out with her IV cord or something else.

"Could be better, but I can't complain. At least I'm still alive and kicking." Keyanna already heard from Michael about what happened, but she wanted to hear things from Porscha's mouth. When she asked her about it, she practically repeated everything that Michael had already told her. What she didn't understand was why she was so mad at Michael and not showing any feelings toward Devon's actions in any of this.

"I don't know if Michael told you or not, but we are getting a divorce," Porscha rattled off. Keyanna's neck snapped back as she turned her head towards Porscha.

"Say that again."

"Michael and I are getting a divorce. What part of that didn't you get? I can't deal with someone that I can't trust and who apparently can't trust me."

"Maybe it's the medication talking, but I don't see you or Michael separating, let alone divorcing. You've been together too long to just end it so abruptly," Keyanna reasoned.

"Who said anything about it being abruptly? It's been a long time coming. He doesn't know how to treat me, he doesn't please me sexually, and we're broke. Yeah, you heard me. We are broke!" Porscha repeated. "I don't even know how I didn't see the shit coming. The signs were there, and I kept overlooking them because I loved his punk ass, but he won't ever get me like that again. I bet the next man I end up with is going to catch hell trying to hide bank statements and shit from me," Porscha ranted. For the first time, Keyanna was speechless. She didn't know what to say to her friend. She didn't even believe that nothing she said would be enough to comfort Porscha at such a tough time.

"Wow, I don't know what to say," Keyanna honestly admitted.

"You don't have to say anything. I've been such a horrible friend to you; you didn't deserve that. I don't know how I'm going to make it up to you, but I promise you that I will. I don't want to lose my sister," Porscha advised her.

"Stop being a crybaby; you aren't going to lose me. We were having a moment. We will bounce back from it like we always do." Even though Keyanna had told Porscha that, she wasn't sure if she believed that herself.

"I love you, sis."

"I love you too, ole crazy ass girl," Keyanna joked before finally taking a seat next to Porscha so that they could talk a little more.

Just like that, the two women were back to where they started from. Or were they?

### Chapter Twenty-Eight:

With Michael gone and Keyanna in the back visiting with Porscha, Devon took the opportunity to reach out to Agent Caldwell. He felt guilty about what happened to Porscha and wanted to make things right. The only way he could think to do that was to call them off from pursuing Michael.

Devon surveyed the waiting room before taking baby DJ into the bathroom. He quickly shut the door and then checked the three stalls inside to make sure nobody was in there with him. When he saw that it was all clear, he pushed the heavy metal trash can behind the door so that he could hear someone before they came in and to hopefully keep people out of there.

He sat the car seat down and swiftly snatched his phone out of his pocket. He dialed back to the number that Agent Caldwell had called him from earlier.

"What's up, bro?" Agent Caldwell answered the phone.

"I need to talk to you," Devon announced.

"Talk to me about what?"

"Reginald, stop questioning me and tell me where I can meet you at," Devon sternly demanded.

"I'm in the parking garage. Come out to the third row on the first level and make sure you aren't being followed," Agent Caldwell directed.

**Bam... Bam...**

"What the fuck?" Devon heard someone say as the bathroom door hit up against the trash can he'd put behind it. He almost dropped his phone when he heard the noise.

"What the fuck is that?" Agent Caldwell questioned.

"Someone trying to come in the bathroom. I'll be out in a few," Devon replied before ending the call. He rushed over to the trash can and moved it out of the way.

"Do I need to call security? What the hell are you doing in here?" Someone from housekeeping was trying to get inside the bathroom." Devon assumed that it was time for it to be cleaned.

"My bad, I was trying to change my lil' man and didn't want anybody walking in on us," Devon lied.

"If you would've gone into the last stall, you would've known that there was a changing table in there. Don't block this door again. If a Fire Marshal would've came in here, you would've been in serious trouble." Devon felt like the man was scolding him, and it was irritating him.

"Look, I told your ass I was sorry. Don't come talking to me like you're my damn daddy or that you own this fuckin' hospital," Devon barked and pushed past the man. He didn't want to hear anything else the man had to say.

Devon peeked around the waiting area before making a dash for the exit. He had to make sure Keyanna and Michael were nowhere around to follow him out to see Agent Caldwell. He took his time walking to the parking garage, being sure to keep checking his surroundings every step of the way.

**Beep...**

The sound of a horn blowing caused Devon to abruptly look up. He'd managed to be standing next to Agent Caldwell's car and didn't even notice. Agent Caldwell motioned for him to come join him in the car. Devon looked around once more before opening the back door on the passenger side to the Maroon Chevy Impala that Agent Caldwell was driving. He slid DJ's car seat onto the peanut butter leather seats and strapped him in before lightly closing the door behind him. He didn't want to make too much noise and risk waking DJ up.

"So, that's your little one?" Agent Caldwell asked once Devon had gotten in the front seat on the passenger side. He glanced back at DJ and smiled before refocusing his attention on Devon.

"Yeah, but that's not what I wanted to talk to you about. We need to drop this shit with Michael. He's not the one that you need to be going after."

"Are you out of your fuckin' mind?" Agent Caldwell scoffed.

"No, I'm being logical. Look at where we're at. I've already fucked up his life enough, which is what my aim was from the jump. If you want that Deuce character or that J-Dubb nigga, then get them. But, leave Michael alone, Reginald."

"I'm going to act like your ass has been drinking because there is no way that nigga is going to walk away from this shit. He has been doing dirt for years and will have to pay for it." He paused. "He called me the other day," Agent Caldwell confessed.

"For what? What did he say?" Devon quizzed.

"He said that he was willing to work with me. He has no idea that me telling him to work with me to stay out of jail was all a lie. He's going to have to do time for his part in all of this."

"Well, I don't want shit else to do with it. I fucked up even getting involved from the jump."

"Stop acting like you give a damn about Michael."

"I do," Devon spoke. He wasn't sure if he was trying to convince himself or Agent Caldwell of the lie.

"You must've forgotten that I know you. Not only that, but I've been following Michael, his wife, and your ass. It's not him that you're worried about. It's his wife that you've been fuckin' behind his back," Agent Caldwell discussed. Devon looked up as if he'd seen a ghost. "What? You didn't think I'd find out? Come on, we're the Feds; we find out everything."

"Why the fuck y'all following me? I don't have shit to do with what the hell he got going on? My damn company is legit," Devon snarled.

"Yeah, but we had to be sure. How was we supposed to know that you weren't working with him to help him clean up that drug money? At the end of the day, yeah, you're my friend. But, I have a job to do."

"In other words, you would've taken me down just to do your damn job?" Devon was furious. He should've never gotten involved. He realized how much he'd fucked up at that point.

"Just be thankful that we don't have to worry about that. You're good as far as I'm concerned. I can understand you wanting to be out of this situation, and that's fine. You've done all that you could've done anyways. It's in our hands now."

"What does that mean?"

"It means that your services are no longer needed. You can go back to trying to live your life; if that's even possible. Just know that we are going to be taking Michael down sooner rather than later." Hearing those words caused Devon to shudder a bit. The chills running down his spine bothered him. "Man, I know that you think this is messed up; especially, with you working with us. But you really haven't done anything if that makes you feel better. You agreed to come visit with them to see what you can find out from inside the home, but you haven't given us anything. All of the information and evidence we have against him is what we accumulated on our own. That should help you clear your conscious."

"Well, it doesn't. I shouldn't have ever gotten involved with this shit," Devon barked.

"Stop beating yourself up; you ain't do shit. I don't know how many times you want me to say that shit to you," Agent Caldwell fussed.

"Whatever." Devon had heard more than enough. He jumped out of the car and moved toward the back door. He yanked it open in order to retrieved DJ.

"Hold on, Devon. I need to tell you something."

"Seems to me you only have a few seconds to talk. So, what is it?" Devon questioned as he unsnapped DJ from the back seat.

"It's about your wife," Agent Caldwell confessed. Before he could say another word, Devon cut him off.

"Whatever you got to say about my wife, keep it to yourself. I didn't give you permission to follow her or me. You violated my privacy, and that was fucked up considering the fact that I was willingly working with you. Keep anything you have to say about me or her to your fuckin' self," Devon barked. He slammed the back door after he'd taken DJ out and stormed back toward the emergency room.

Devon figured that at some point, his involvement with everything was going to come out. He contemplated over whether or not he needed to go ahead and reveal his part in it to Keyanna, Porscha, and Michael, but he couldn't. He didn't care how Michael and Porcha viewed him, but he didn't want Keyanna to look at him any differently. She was his wife. The love of his life. The only woman he'd trust to fight for him when he could no longer fight for himself.

By the time Devon made it back inside of the hospital, Keyanna was standing in the waiting area with an angry expression on her face.

"Where the hell have you been?" She walked up on him.

"I was taking DJ out of here for a while because it's so noisy," he lied. He didn't know what else to say, and he certainly didn't want to make her act a damn fool in that emergency room and they ended up being escorted out of there.

"I'm about to leave."

"Where are you going?"

"I'm going to check into a hotel."

"What happened to you not wanting to take the baby to a hotel?" Devon questioned her. He found himself becoming upset because, had they stayed in a hotel from the jump, they could've avoided all of the bullshit they endured the past few days.

"Seems that we don't have a choice at this point. Too much has happened at that house for me to want to stay there," she explained.

"What about me?"

"What about you?"

"Where am I supposed to go?"

"Take your ass back to the house," she nonchalantly instructed. By that time, she'd taken DJ's car seat from Devon's hand and sat it on the chair closest to her. Devon watched as she unsnapped DJ and checked his diaper. He was still resting like a nigga that had just gotten home from a twelve-hour shift.

"Why you bothering him? Let him sleep," Devon commented.

"That shows who's the most involved parent. He can't just sit in piss and shit or he'll get a diaper rash. Furthermore, he has to eat every so many hours. If that means me waking him up, then so be it," she snapped at him.

"Can't you wait until we get to the hotel. Then you can get him ready for bed and I can run out to get us something to eat."

"We who? Who said you were going with us?"

"Come on, Key. Why you doing this shit? You keep trying to divide our family like I've done something so bad. Then you've been accusing me of cheating when I ain't done shit but go to work and come back home. Maybe you're the one out there with another nigga," Devon suggest.

"Humph..." Keyanna returned. Devon felt as if his blood was about to boil. *Is this bitch telling me that she fuckin' around on me?* Devon thought to himself.

"What the fuck is that supposed to mean? Don't piss me off, Keyanna," Devon growled.

"Don't ask me no questions, and I won't tell you no lies. Did I say that right?" Keyanna used the same line on him that he'd said to her that caused her to want to divorce his ass. He didn't know how to take it.

"I said don't fuckin' play with me, Keyanna, and I meant that shit." Devon walked up on her, invading her persona space. "Tell me the truth. Are you fuckin' off?"

"Boy bye," Keyanna quipped and mushed his forehead. He grabbed ahold of her hand and was about to twist it until DJ started squirming in his seat. Keyanna had a look on her face that he'd never seen before. It was one of fear. He never wanted her to feel like she had to be afraid of him.

"I'm sorry. I don't know what came over me. I just can't think of you being with someone other than me," he apologized to her.

"Do unto others as you'd have them do unto you," she told him. He knew all too well what that meant. *Does she really know that I had cheated on her more than the one time I told her about?* He thought.

"Can I at least stay with you and our son tonight? I don't want to be alone and I don't feel comfortable with y'all being out here alone," he sincerely spoke. Keyanna stood there for a minute. "Please," he pleaded with her.

"Fine. But we are getting double beds, and if you try anything, you will find yourself getting put the fuck out," she warned him. The look on her face showed that she meant business.

Devon was fully aware that he'd fucked up with Keyanna. He didn't know what it would take to make things right, but he was willing to try anything. There was no way he was going to live the rest of his life without her in it.

### Chapter Twenty-Nine:

Porscha was transferred to a regular room around seven o'clock that evening. She was hungry and tired. Michael had made it back with an overnight bag for the both of them. She wanted to tell him to leave, but she really didn't want to be in the room by herself.

"You okay?" he asked her, interrupting her thoughts.

"Yep." She was very short with him.

"Porscha, if you want me to leave, then say so. If not, then you are going to have to treat me a little better than what the fuck you are doing now," Michael demanded. She glimpsed up at him and was about to put him in his place, but she couldn't. The sadness that consumed his face showed her a wounded man. She couldn't bring herself to hurting him more than he was already hurting inside.

"I'm sorry," she apologized. She wasn't sorry for confronting him the way that she did. She was sorry for how she did it and when she did it. Her initial plan was to tie him down to the hotel bed and torture him a bit before asking for a divorce, but God had other plans. She realized that when she ended up at the hospital. She felt as though she received her karma early.

"Sorry for what?"

"Don't push it. Be glad you got that much of an apology out of me. Now, can you please go get me something to eat?" she asserted.

"Yeah. I'm going to have to get you something from within the hospital because you know that I didn't bring the car. Keyanna is gonna pick us up in the morning."

"We can just use Uber Eats."

"I forgot all about that. Let me pull the app up," he told her. Michael pulled out his phone and started scrolling through it. "I'm going to have to step outside of the hospital. My damn signal is not good at all in here. Do you know what you have a taste for?"

"Get me some crabs from Bluff City Crab. Get me the boss bag, spicy, and extra juicy. Make sure it has the Memphis mix. Oh, and can you at least go get me two cokes from the vending machine?"

"Two cokes? What the hell you need two cokes for?"

"Helloooo.... I ordered spicy crabs, and it's in the boss bag. I'm about to be as full as a tic."

"Aight. I got you, baby," Michael responded and winked at Porscha. For once in a long time, she didn't feel disgusted by the thought of her husband touching her or showing her any type of emotions."

Michael stood from the seat he'd been occupying next to her bed and moved over to her. He stared into her eyes rather intently for what seemed like forever. She had to blink a few times because it started to mess with her vision the way he was looking at her. It seemed like he was reading her soul, and she didn't know how to feel about that.

"Porscha, I know I fucked up. I promise I'm going to make things better. I wasted years trying to cover up for the way I'd been screwing up our money. If you really knew the things I was doing to keep us afloat, you would see how much I love you and want to make you happy."

"Can we not talk about this now? We are having a good moment, and I want to keep it that way. Let's just enjoy the night," she insisted. She didn't know how to feel and was going to need some time to think about what she wanted to happen with them. What she did know was that they were having a great night and she didn't want to mess it up thinking about anything negative.

"Okay, baby. Let me go order the food. I'll be right back," he told her.

Michael left out of the room. Porscha sat up in her bed and grabbed her cell phone off the table that was beside her. She saw that she had a few texts and a missed call. She opted to return the call before responding to any of the text.

"You called?" she spoke as soon as the other person answered.

"Yeah. I just wanted to make sure you were okay."

"I'm fine for now. Where are you?"

"At the crib."

"Why didn't you come see me?"

"Porscha, how was I going to see you when both Michael and Keyanna were there. They were going to suspect something if I acted too determined to see you."

"Who gives a fuck? We've been curving their asses for years and hiding our feelings for one another. My marriage is over, and according to Keyanna, yours is too. We can finally be together," Porscha happily suggested.

"No, that can't happen. I don't want to lose my wife and son," Devon refuted.

"Fuck you mean? You told me that you wanted to be with me. Why the hell are things different now? What has she done to make you want to stay with her now? You don't even want that damn baby."

"Stop questioning me. I only called to see if you were okay and clearly you are. Enjoy the rest of your night." Devon was getting ready to hang up the phone.

"Wait!" Porscha hollered.

Porscha had stood from her bed and was pacing back and forth in the room. She was sick and tired of being sick and tired. In that moment, she thought she was stupid. She was fully aware of how women tried to take men from their homes. She was also aware of the fact that she signed on to be a side bitch. She didn't ever expect to catch feelings for him. But, now that she had them, she couldn't shake them.

"What do you want?" Devon quizzed.

"All I want is to see you. Can you make that happen?"

"I'll see you when you get to the house tomorrow. Right now, I'm trying to make shit up to my wife, so I can keep my family together," he explained.

"Where is all of this coming from?" Porscha put her right hand on her forehead. She'd suddenly acquired a headache. It had everything to do with the bad news she was hearing from Devon. She didn't agree to the shit one bit.

"Devon, can you tend to your son so I can take a shower?" Porscha heard Keyanna in the background and could feel her blood starting to boil. Her body was heating up. If she had a heart monitor on, it would've gone berserk because the way her heart was racing.

"You're with her?"

"She's my wife."

"Fuck that bitch!" Porscha smack.

"No, fuck you, bitch. Don't ever disrespect my wife or my damn seed again, and I mean that shit, Porscha. I'll come to the hospital, snatch that IV out of your arm, and stab your fuckin' ass in the eye with the needle. Don't try me, hoe," Devon roared.

Porscha threw her phone up against the wall and let out a gut-wrenching scream. She couldn't believe the way that Devon had talked to her and had made her feel like she was lower than low.

Resentment. That was the only word that could describe the way she felt. Michael loved her, but it wasn't the way that Devon loved her. The only time Michael even thought to tell her that he loved her was when they had gotten into it.

*Knock...*

After one knock on the door, a nurse came waltzing inside of her room. Porscha turned around with a look of distress on her face. The nurse's face turned whiter than it already was. She jogged toward Porscha and tried to assist her with sitting back in the bed, but Porscha pushed her away.

"Stop!" Porscha demanded.

"I need you to sit down and calm down. What is going on?" the nurse asked.

"Bitch, I don't know you like that to be telling you my mufuckin' business," Porscha told her through clenched teeth. She was full of aggression.

"I'm sorry. I'm just trying to get you to calm down. You have these machines going crazy in here?"

"What damn machines? The only thing that's hooked to me is the IV," Porscha asserted. She checked out the machines in the room to make sure she wasn't tripping before peering back at the nurse. "Who the hell are you anyways? You aren't the same nurse that I had earlier."

"We had a shift change. I'm Lucinda. I'll be the nurse with you for the next twelve hours," Nurse Lucinda explained.

"The lies you tell. I'm getting out of here first thing in the morning," Porscha muttered.

"We do have you down to discharge tomorrow, but that's pending the results of the tests they ran on you. Also, the doctor will have to come by and see you first. Then, you can be discharged. That will probably be around noon time, which is more than twelve hours away from now," Nurse Lucinda refuted.

"Whatever. You can leave my room now," Porscha spat. Nurse Lucinda stood straight up. She glared down at Porscha. Porscha started to feel some type of way by the way the woman was looking at her. It seemed like Nurse Lucinda was trying her.

"Hey, baby!" Michael walked in. "They are su—" Michael stopped mid-sentence when he saw that there was someone else in the room with them. "Hi, I'm Michael," he told the nurse. Michael extended his hands out for her to shake, but Porscha jumped up and slapped his hand down.

"Nurse, Michael. Michael, nurse," she half-assed introduced them.

"Why you smack my hand down?" Michael asked in a state of confusion.

"She got two hands; she don't need your shit," Porscha rattled off and rolled her eyes. She moved back over toward the bed as if nothing happened.

"I'll leave you two alone to talk," Nurse Lucinda spoke. She was getting ready to leave out the room, but Michael threw his hand up to stop her.

"You're the nurse on duty this shift?"

"Yes!"

"She didn't like that too much?"

"Not at all."

"Why? What happened that made her so upset?"

"I came in to introduce myself, and she was already upset. I tried to assist her with sitting on the bed, but she just started going off on me," Nurse Lucinda commented.

"I'm so sorry about that. We've had a rough past couple of days. I'm sure she took her anger for someone else out on you. Please accept my apology," Michael insisted.

"Fuck are you doing? I didn't tell you to apologize to her. I know damn well what I was doing. Now stop talking to the bitch so she can leave."

"You know what, I'm going to see if I can get someone else to deal with her. I'm not going to work twelve hours with someone being rude and disrespecting me," Nurse Lucinda asserted. Michael was gearing up to say something else, but Porscha stopped him.

"Let her go," Porscha instructed. Michael mouth to Nurse Lucinda that he was sorry. She shook her head and left out of the room.

"What was that all about?" Michael probed.

"We were doing good. Don't come in here asking me no fuckin' questions. I don't like the bitch."

"You don't even know her," Michael announced. Porscha turned her head and looked down. She was looking for something. Picking up the remote, she turned the television back up and began to search for something to watch. "You really doing this?" Michael asked. He surveyed the room and noticed Porscha's phone in a corner. That raised a red flag to him. She had to be talking to someone on the phone that made her mad. He slowly strolled over to where the phone was and picked it up. If it weren't for the otter box on the phone, it would've been shattered to pieces.

"I'm going down to get the food. I'll be back," Michael stated. Porscha nodded her head and continued to focus on the television.

Michael took Porscha's phone out of the room with him. She was trying her best to ignore him, so she never realized what he'd done. But she was surely going to pay for it later.

### *Chapter Thirty:*

Michael noted the way that Porscha was acting when he returned to the room. When he saw her phone lying on the floor, he realized that it had to be because of someone she'd just finished talking to. He took her phone with him when he left out the room. Porscha didn't even think about it, which was good for him.

Walking down the hall to wait out front for the food to arrive, he put in the passcode he last remembered her having on her phone. After three failed attempts, the phone locked. He was aware that he couldn't try it again because each time you tried, the phone locked again, and the time for you to make another attempt would be longer and longer.

"Fuck!" he mumbled.

"You okay?" the woman next to him asked. Michael was so into trying to get into the phone that he hadn't realize if anyone was by him or not.

"I'm good. Family shit!" Michael replied.

"Could you please watch your mouth? I don't use that type of language around my children," the woman told him. Michael looked down and saw that the woman had four young children with her. Three girls and one boy.

"My bad; I didn't even know anybody was around me. I apologize to your shorties for my language," Michael apologized.

"Thank you," the woman told him.

*Michael pulled his phone out and shot Keyanna a text.*

*Michael: Aye! They moved the devil to room 319.*

*Keyanna: Okay. Anything come back from her tests yet?*

*Michael: Naw. I guess we will find out something tomorrow. You still picking us up, right?*

*Keyanna: Yeah, I'll be up there around eleven.*

*Michael: Cool.*

Michael was about to text something else but stopped. He somewhat felt bad for what he was about to ask her, but he had to get into Porscha's phone. He needed to find out who she'd been talking to that made her so mad that she had to throw the damn phone.

"Fuck it!" he said to himself before texting Keyanna again.

*Michael: Do you happen to have the password to get into her phone?*

*Keyanna: Why would I have that? We're close, but not that damn close. I don't even let Devon have my passcode and he's my husband.*

Michael laughed because he knew how she felt. He and Porscha had always been open with each other, for the most part, but there were some things that they kept to themselves. Their individual bank account information and their passcode to their phones were just a few of those things.

"I see someone's in a better mood," the woman said to him.

"Yeah, I'm good. Sorry about earlier," Michael apologized again.

"It's all good," the woman returned.

They were standing in front of the elevator, waiting for it to take them down to the first floor.

"Who are you visiting?" the woman asked Michael. It was clear that she was trying to make small talk. If Michael didn't know any better, he'd think that she was flirting with him.

"Huh?"

"Who do you have in the hospital?"

"Oh, I'm here for my cousin. She got into a fight and got knocked out," he partially told the truth.

"I'm sorry to hear that."

"What about you? Who'd you come here to see?"

"My mother is here. She got sick about two days ago and has been here ever since. I've been considering sending her to another hospital because they haven't told us much."

"Yeah, I'd be looking into that myself. Nobody plays about their mother," Michael joked, causing the woman to giggle.

"What's your name?" the woman inquired.

"Michael. Yours?"

"Ginger."

"Nice to meet you, Ginger." Michael outstretched his arm and extended his hand to receive hers. Ginger placed her soft hand inside of Michael's. He shook her hand and smiled at her.

Ginger returned the smile. "Who are these little ones?" Michael asked, referring to Ginger's children.

"This is Ana, Mo'Nique, Rose, and Ross." It wasn't until she told Michael their names that he noticed that she had a set of twins.

"That's a lot of girls," he commented.

"Yeah. Girls run in my family," Ginger informed him.

"So, you mean if you and I were to have one together, we'd be having a girl?" Michael was very forward with Ginger. That was how he was with every woman that he was with. It wasn't because he was trying to get over on them. It was the fact that he was trying to keep everything straight from the jump. He'd fuck with you, but you better know that he wasn't leaving home for no damn body. Porscha had his heart, and even though he didn't do right by her, he didn't want to live his life without her. Besides, she was stepping out on him so what they did was no different.

"Naw. I'm done with babies."

"Say what nih?" Michael frowned up at Ginger. Just that quick he'd lost interest in talking to her.

"What you frowning like that for? I have four kids. I don't want or need anymore," Ginger advised him.

"That's cool. Hopefully, my wife will give me some soon," Michael quipped.

"Your wife? How the hell were you just trying to talk to me if you have a whole wife at home."

"My whole wife is actually in the hospital, which is why I'm here. I'll get at you later," Michael chided and walked away from Ginger.

Michael got away from Ginger as fast as he could. He needed to be outside when their food arrived. The whole time he was walking away, he could hear her cussing at him and calling him all kinds of names. He chuckled because she had just told him to watch his mouth around her kids, but then she had the nerve to be talking crazy to him.

By the time Michael reached the front of the hospital, the Uber Eats driver had arrived with their order. He gave the man a $5 tip. The driver looked down at the tip and frowned.

"What?" Michael asked.

"This all you got?" the driver returned.

"Be grateful you got that because I normally don't give tips."

"Mannnn, you have damn near a $200 order," the driver grunted.

"You right," Michael stated and snatched the $5 bill out of the driver's hand. "Ungrateful ass," he barked and walked back inside the hospital.

Michael headed to the cafeteria so he could get them something out of the vending machine to drink. People were staring at him as he walked throughout the hospital. He knew it had something to do with the fish smell that was coming from the bags he had in his hand. He didn't care because he was about to eat good. He didn't even try to speak to anyone else around him. He got their drinks and high-stepped all the way back to Porscha's room.

### Chapter Thirty-One:

With Michael out of the room, Porscha decided she wanted to call Devon back. She had to make things right with him because he'd become her everything, and he didn't know it yet.

Dragging her IV pole behind her, Porscha marched over to the corner where she'd thrown her phone. She searched for it and was upset when she couldn't find it. It dawned on her that Michael had to have taken her phone because it didn't come up missing until after he had left. Then, she thought about the nurse coming into her room. She stormed back over toward her bed. She picked up her remote and hit the red button to call the nurse.

Two seconds after she hit the button, she became antsy. Nobody answered her. She hit it another three times before someone finally came over the intercom over her bed.

"May we help you?"

"You can help me by losing the attitude and sending Nurse Bitch back in here," Porscha demanded.

"Ma'am, we don't have a nurse in here by the name, and I don't have an attitude. I'll send someone in there to help you," the woman told Porscha.

"No, send me my nurse. Don't send me no damn body else or I'm going to shut this mufuckin' hospital down," Porscha grumbled.

Right after the intercom beeped, letting Porscha know that the woman was no longer listening to her, Michael stepped back inside the room.

"You okay?" he asked Porscha.

"No, the nurse stole my fuckin' phone," Porscha fumed.

"Nobody stole your phone. I have it," Michael confirmed.

"What the hell are you doing with my phone?" Porscha held her hand out for Michael to hand it to her.

"Because when I was walking out the door, I saw it lying on the floor in the corner. I picked it up and took it with me when I went to get the food. Plus, it couldn't have been too important for you to have for you to throw it in the corner the way that you did," Michael explained.

"Shut up and give me my phone. You don't even know why I threw it," Porcha muttered and held her hand out to receive her phone.

"I'm sure it had everything to do with one of the niggas you've been fuckin' with behind my back."

"I told you that I've never cheated on you. Just because you saw how men come at me doesn't mean I opened my legs for them."

"Your ass didn't tell them that you had a husband or stop them from talking to you like you were a two-dollar whore either."

"What the fuck did you just say to me?" Porscha stood from her bed. She grabbed ahold of her IV pole and pulled it behind her as she made her way toward her husband.

"Porscha, I'm not about to do this shit with you. Get the fuck out of my face and sit the fuck down. We can deal with this shit at home. Right now, I'm about to sit down and enjoy my fuckin' food," Michael roared. Porscha stared Michael up and down. By the look on his face, she knew she'd made him mad. But she wasn't letting up until she got her phone back from him.

"Hand me my phone!" she instructed with her hand still held out.

*Knock... Knock...*

There was a knock on the door. Porscha was sure it was just the nurse coming back to see what she wanted. She called her, but now that she knew Michael had her phone, she had no use for her to step in her room.

"Go away!' she yelled.

"We are with security, ma'am," a male's voice spoke.

"See, you done fucked around and made them call security on you," Michael blurted out. "You do realize they can refuse service to you."

"No, the hell they can't. I can sue them if they do."

Michael got quiet. She figured it was because he no longer wanted to fight with her. She didn't blame him. If she were him, she'd shut up to because everyone knew that trying to win a fight against her was pointless.

***Knock... Knock...***

Hearing them knock again, she knew she had no choice but to go ahead and open the door. She suddenly became nervous. While she said that they couldn't refuse services to her, she knew that they could kick her out of the hospital like anyone else.

"Don't let them put me out," she pleaded with Michael.

"You're a big girl; you can handle yourself," Michael chided and walked back over to the chair that was by her bed and took a seat. Porscha's eyes stayed trained on him the entire time. She couldn't believe the man that was supposed to protect her was hurting her so bad and showing her that he didn't give a damn what happened to her.

"You really going to let them put me out of here?"

"I'll tell you what... If you can admit that you had an abortion and not a miscarriage, then I'll help you," Michael carped.

"Abortion? What are you talking about?" Porscha's mouth fell open. She'd given herself away, but she had to find a way to recover. "Huh? Who had an abortion? I had a damn miscarriage!" she affirmed.

"Yeah, and I got a ten-inch dick. When you're ready to tell the truth, then we can talk about me helping you," Michael condemned.

"But h-h-h-how did you find out?" She was caught. There was no reason for her to continue to play crazy.

"I told you that I went through your phone. I found a lot of messages, even the messages you had in that secret folder. But, don't worry, your secret is safe with me.

Michael stood from his chair. He went over to the sink that was by the door of the room. He put their food down on the counter along with the drinks. He put the drinks inside the bags and opened the door.

"Where are you going with my food? I'm hungry," Porscha barked.

"Let your baby daddy get you something to eat," Michael returned and left out the room.

Porscha immediately felt sick to her stomach. She tried to play Michael when she found out his secrets, but the shit had backfired on her. Now, she was fucked like Chuck. She didn't know what she was going to do. All she could hope for was that he didn't know who the real father of her baby was.

### Chapter Thirty-Two:

"Bitch!" Devon spat as Keyanna was walking out of the bathroom with a sleepy DJ in her arms.

"What's the matter?" she inquired.

"I'm just ready to go back home and get our lives back in order. I knew coming up here was a bad idea," he commented. He noted the way that Porscha was acting and how she ended their call. Something told him that she'd grown tired of dealing with being his side chick and was going to tell Keyanna the truth about them.

"It's okay. If things are meant to be, they will be. As of now, I don't see things going back to the way that they used to be. Too much has happened and too much has been revealed," Keyanna admitted.

"Baby, don't think like that. We have to remain positive. I love you, and I will die before I lose you," Devon asserted.

"Well, if you have plans on taking your life, make sure it's just yours that you take."

"What do you mean by that?"

"Exactly what the hell I said. I don't have time for that 'if I can't have you, no one else will,' shit. People be trying to kill the next person for wanting to walk away from them when they were the cause of them walking away in the first place," she acknowledged.

"Do you really think all of this is my fault?"

"No, I think we both played an intricate role in what happened between us. What I'm saying is that if you on some suicidal bullshit because we may be done, then it don't need to be a suicide-homicide."

"I would never do anything to hurt you."

"Come again? You do realize what has happened over the past few days, right?"

"You know what I meant, Keyanna. Now, the problems that we have can be fixed. I was mad and said some fucked up shit to you. I can admit that I was wrong. People say shit when they are angry, and you know that. That's exactly what happened," he pleaded with her.

Keyanna pushed past Devon to get to the bed. She picked up some of the pillows off the bed and made a square in the middle of the bed with the pillows. She gently laid DJ between the pillows, on his back.

"He's going to fall," Devon barked. He noticed that Keyanna's body jerked when he spoke so loud to her. "My bad; I didn't mean to scare you. I'm just worried that he's going to fall off the bed."

"He's not even rolling over yet, so he'll be fine," Keyanna assured him.

"Well, why you lay him on his back? Nobody sleeps good on their back but dead folks."

"Stop it, Devon!"

"Stop what?"

"Stop acting like you give a damn about him. Since the day he was born, you've barely held him or acknowledged him. I'm not stupid. I know you don't want him, which is another reason that we can't stay together. He's here, and he's not going anywhere. I'd never subject my son to being around someone that can't accept the fact that he is a major blessing," Keyanna expressed. Devon stood before her with his mouth gapped open. Keyanna waited for him to say something in response, but he had nothing to say. Keyanna was right. Devon thought he did a damn good job hiding the way he felt about DJ. Clearly, he didn't or else Keyanna wouldn't be able to say the things that she said.

"It's not that I don't want him. It's jus—"

"It's just what?" she interrupted him.

"I know how couples change once a baby is involved. Look at us now. Ever since he's been here, we've done nothing but argue, and I'm tired of it. I just want things to be the way they were before he came."

"That's when you compromise. We make time for each other. We help each other with the baby so that we can have breaks and refocus on ourselves. I know having a baby is a lot, but so is being in a relationship. They both take time, communication, and commitment. If you can't do that, then there's no point of us even having this conversation."

"Who said I couldn't do it? I know I can. All I'm asking is that you give me another chance. I don't want to lose my family. Please," he begged her.

Devon took things a step further. He walked over to his suitcase that they stopped by Porscha's house to grab on the way to their hotel. When he got to it, he unzipped the small part in the front and pulled out a little box. Keyanna had stopped paying him attention and was focusing on finding her something to sleep in. Michael stood behind her and dropped down to one knee. When Keyanna turned around, she started screaming and tears instantly fell from her eyes. Devon grabbed Keyanna's left hand with his right hand and gazed into her eyes.

"I wanted to do this at a better time, but I feel like now is the time for me to do it. I love you, Keyanna. I know I fucked up along the way, but I swear I'm willing to spend the rest of my life making things up to you. Please don't give up on me... on us."

Keyanna did the unthinkable. She snatched her hand away from him. Devon's eyes grew big as hell and were suddenly bloodshot red.

"What the fuck!" he bellowed. "What are you doing?" he roared.

"You think that asking me to marry you again is going to fix this shit? Maybe it'll work on some stupid ass bitch or the bitch you were on the phone with while I was in the bathroom, taking care of *our son*, but it won't work on me." Keyanna snatched her purse and keys off the sofa that was in the room and ran out the door.

Devon was confused. Why would she start crying and screaming if she weren't happy about him proposing to her? It didn't make any sense. He stood to go after her, but DJ started fussing. He had to decide if he was going to be selfish and go after his wife or be selfless and take care of his son. For once, he did the right thing and went to tend to DJ.

### Chapter Thirty-Three:

When Porscha was released from the hospital, Keyanna was there to drive them home. Michael hated the fact that the entire car ride was done in silence. He wasn't used to it. He and Porscha were still mad at each other, but he wasn't going to let Keyanna or anyone else know why. If Porscha wanted to keep up the lie that she had a miscarriage, he was going to let her do so. However, he wasn't going to be standing by her side while she did.

Arriving at home, he assisted Porscha with going inside. He tucked her away in the bed and went to get her bag out of the SUV. He noticed Keyanna still sitting in the SUV. He couldn't help but to ask her what was wrong.

"You good, Key?"

"Just thinking and trying to process everything that has happened. This trip was not supposed to go like this."

"I know, and I hate that things went down the way that they did. It's really all my fault. When Porscha was having all of those dreams, I should've confessed and told her everything. It's just that I thought I would be able to make enough money to make shit right before she found out, ya know?" Michael's phone vibrated in his pocket while he spoke. He pulled it out and realized it was the same number Deuce called him from the night before trying to meet up with him. Because he was having an intimate moment with Keyanna, which rarely happened, and because he didn't want to be bothered with Deuce and his bullshit, he chose not to answer.

"So, you're broke?" Keyanna flat out asked him. He knew she already knew the answer to that, but he answered her anyways because he didn't want to cause another argument if she thought he was trying to ignore her or if he said something smart to her.

"I wouldn't say that we are broke, but I owe a lot of money to different people and bills. If I don't handle it, my ass will be sitting behind bars for some shit," Michael revealed.

"You may want to answer your phone; it keeps vibrating; it must be important," Keyanna announced. Michael didn't think she heard the vibration, but he was wrong. She looked irritated too.

"No, it's work calling. I can deal with them another time. Right now, I need to make sure Porscha is good and see what I can do about my money problems. I can't go to jail. Shit, I won't go to jail. What the fuck I look like being behind bars?"

"Behind bars for what? You keep saying that, but there are a lot of people that don't pay their bills and end up losing shit, but I've never known them to be put in jail behind it," Keyanna remarked.

Michael realized that he was about to reveal to Keyanna what he really did. He caught himself because he didn't want to get anyone else involved in his bullshit.

***Tap... Tap...***

There was a tap on Keyanna's window. Michael saw her reaching down in search of something. When she pulled out a shiny pink Ruger, he grabbed his chest. He caught a glimpse of who was tapping on the window and wished that Keyanna would've just pulled the trigger. There Deuce stood with a mean mug on his face and his phone to his ear while Michael's phone continued to buzz.

"Who the fuck are you?" Keyanna asked, cracking her window a little.

"I'm Deuce. I'm here to have a little talk with Michael."

"You know him?" Keyanna questioned Michael. "I've never seen him before and you've never mentioned him as being one of your clients, friends, or family."

"Keyanna, you just got up here. You don't know everybody I know or that I work with," Michael reminded her.

Keyanna sat still for a minute then glanced back at a sleeping DJ.

"Can we sit in your truck to talk? I don't like talking business in the house around Porscha."

"Sure," Keyanna obliged. She slid the gun back under the seat and got out of the SUV. Michael helped her with getting DJ out of the vehicle. He told Deuce he'd be right back and carried DJ inside for Keyanna.

When Michael returned, Deuce was sitting on the passenger's side of the SUV. He shook his head and trudged toward the driver's side. He leisurely slid inside, but he kept his door open in case he needed to make a quick exit.

"What are you doing showing up at my house like this? I told you I would reach out to you," Michael grumbled. Deuce chuckled.

"Nigga, didn't I tell your punk ass that you don't run shit. Everything happens by my damn rules. You better get that shit through your thick ass skull," Deuce gawked. He took it a step further when he used his index finger and poked Michael in the side of the head.

"What are you doing here? I need to go make sure my wife is okay."

"That's right, she did just get out of the hospital. Is she feeling any better?"

"How the hell do you know about her being in the hospital?"

"I told you that I know everything. You think I don't have people watching your every move? Just like I know that your ass talked to that dumb as federal agent. If I get caught, there will be hell to pay."

"If you get caught, it's because you're being sloppy," Michael announced. "Showing up at my job and now house unannounced are key ways to getting caught. Your ass not even trying to be discreet about the shit."

"Nigga, shut the fuck up," Deuce snapped. He stuck his hand out the window and snapped his fingers twice. Within a matter of seconds, the man that was always with him came strolling up the side of the SUV. He handed Deuce a briefcase and left. Michael peered out the rearview mirror to watch his every move. He noticed him getting inside of a new Lexus.

"Why he sitting there?"

"That's my ride. What, you scared he about to off you?"

"I ain't never scared," Michael lied. He was so scared, his heart was racing.

"I can't tell." Deuce chucked again. "Take this," Deuce instructed and slung the briefcase toward Michael, hitting him in the chest.

"The fuck! Watch it!"

"Or else what?" Deuce growled.

"Look, you not about to keep punking me. If this shit is going to happen, then we are going to do it the right way. What the fuck is this anyway?" Michael probed.

"What the fuck you think it is? You need to clean it, and soon. I'll give you two weeks to get it done," Deuce ordered and stepped out of the car. "And, don't make me have to come find your ass in those two weeks. That will only piss me off, and an angry Deuce ain't good for nobody," Deuce commented.

Michael once again looked in the rearview mirror. He saw Deuce enter the Lexus that was parked on the curb and the car pulled off. It took some time, but Michael was able to regain control of his breathing. He got out of Keyanna's SUV and was about to go inside the house to check on Porscha until he heard sirens nearing his house. He saw swarms of police cars suddenly swoop in around him.

Michael jetted back toward Keyanna's SUV. He watched as the police got out of their cars and pulled their weapons.

"Michael Alexander, step out of the car," he heard Agent Caldwell's voice over the intercom.

"What I do?" Michael yelled out the window.

"We are only here to talk to you," Agent Caldwell responded.

"If you only needed to talk to me, then you could've called or texted me. Hell, you could've sent me an email and asked me to come by the fuckin' station. You brought the gotdamn army to my house, and for what? I'm not going to jail!" Michael screamed. "You hear that? I'm not going to no mufuckin' jail!" he roared.

Porscha, Keyanna, and Devon stood in the front yard. They were trying to figure out what was going on, even though the police were telling them to go back in the house.

"Michael, what the hell are you doing? What is going on here?" He heard Porscha's voice.

"Go back in the house, Porscha. Let me handle this," Michael yelled at her.

"No, get out of that truck, and tell me what's going on now," Porscha demanded. She took it a step further and stomped her feet like that was really going to move him.

"Ma'am, can you come with me?" Agent Caldwell approached Porscha. She glanced over at him like he was a flesh-eating disease. "I'm not going to do anything to hurt you. I just want to talk to you," he explained. It took some convincing before Porscha walked over to the side with Agent Caldwell.

"Leave my wife alone!" Michael jumped out of the SUV with Keyanna's gun in his hand.

"What the fuck? Michael what are you doing with my gun?" Keyanna questioned him. She started toward Michael, but Devon yanked her ass back. "Hey!" she yelled.

"Get the fuck out of the way. Are you trying to get killed?" Devon asked.

"No, but I don't want him to get killed either," she told him.

"Don't nobody care if he gets killed. Nobody told his dumb ass to get out the damn vehicle with a fuckin' gun. If they load his ass up with bullet holes, then that's nobody's fault but his own," Devon refuted.

"You sound so fuckin' stupid. Don't you think we've already had enough black men killed at the hands of the police?"

"That's different. They were innocent. This dummy is asking to be killed," Devon voiced. Keyanna rolled her eyes at him before she refocused her attention back on Michael.

"I'm not going to jail, and the only way you're going to get near me is if I'm dead," Michael warned them. "I told you that I would help you out. I told you that I was willing to help you take that nigga down, and this is how you play me? You come in my neighborhood and embarrass me in front of my family and neighbors! Now, I won't help you do shit!"

"Michael, let me just talk to you," Agent Caldwell stated again.

"Naw, I'm good off you." Michael could see in his peripheral that some of the cops were moving near him. He put the gun up to his head and braced himself.

Everyone in the neighborhood had come out of their homes to see what was going on. Michael wanted to holler at them and tell them to mind the fuckin' business that paid them, but that would've been pointless. As long as the police were there, the spectators were going to be there as well. If a show was what they wanted, a show was what they were going to get.

"Porscha, I love you. Always remember that."

Michael put his hand on the trigger. Closing his eyes, he prepared himself to end it all.

***POW...***

"Nooooo... You can't leave your son without a dad. DJ needs you," Keyanna cried as she went running toward him. But, she was too late...

***(To Be Continued...)***

Pregnant By My Best Friend's Husband

Made in the USA
Las Vegas, NV
16 November 2022

59674687R00152